Regena Andrea Grundy is from Seattle, Washington, and currently lives in Los Angeles, California. This is Regena's first novel; she had no idea that she would ever become an author but it was all God's plan. Regena graduated from Hollywood High School of Performing Arts. After graduating, she studied theatre at AMDA New York City. She later graduated from the Academy of Radio and Television Broadcasting in Huntington Beach, California. She hosts and produces a program with her mother called *Pearls in the Morning* for The Cross TV. Regena has also produced and edited three short films—*In My Front Yard,* which received an honorable mention. *Stories* and *Heel Love,* both projects became winners in The Short Showcase Film festival.

I dedicate this book to Jesus Christ, who is the author and finisher of my faith. To my mommy, Mrs. Joyce Ann Grundy-Green, who is the epitome of a virtuous woman.

Regena Andrea Grundy

DETECTIVE MISTY RIVERS IN "LONG OVERDUE"

AUSTIN MACAULEY PUBLISHERS™

LONDON • CAMBRIDGE • NEW YORK • SHARJAH

Ordering Information
Quantity sales: Special discounts are available on quantity purchases by corporations, associations, and others. For details, contact the publisher at the address below.

Publisher's Cataloging-in-Publication data
Grundy, Regena Andrea
Detective Misty Rivers in "Long Overdue"

ISBN 9781685628819 (Paperback)
ISBN 9781685628826 (ePub e-book)

Library of Congress Control Number: 2023916166

www.austinmacauley.com/us

First Published 2024
Austin Macauley Publishers LLC
40 Wall Street, 33rd Floor, Suite 3302
New York, NY 10005
USA

mail-usa@austinmacauley.com
+1 (646) 5125767

Table of Contents

Chapter 1
The Bloodline

Becoming a detective is the greatest joy and the greatest pain of my life; but the pain is what makes it great. First and foremost, I'm a believer in Jesus Christ; I'm not perfect but *GOD* is. I am Misty Joyce Rivers. I was born in Fayetteville, North Carolina on September 17, 1979. I'm 5'3", slim thick with hot chocolate skin and chestnut brown, fearless eyes. A perfectly round face with baby doll features, medium length thick dark brown semi-curly hair, with small dimples and a smile that would light up your world. When God set me down on this earth, He wasn't joking around. I'm a force for good; get things done, authentic, no-nonsense women. Coming from two generations of law enforcement, it was already written in the stars. My father Detective Andrew Miles Rivers Jr. was born in Fayetteville, North Carolina and his father, my grandpa, was a detective as well. Although back in those days, there was so much racism in Alabama, they only had a select few of colored detectives on the force, but nevertheless, I've heard stories on how my grandpa was a black Sherlock Holmes. His name was Andrew Miles Rivers Sr. born in the rural south of Birmingham, Alabama, in 1925.

My grandpa was a Tuskegee Airmen, and after the war he went on to become a policeman. He was tough, solid and a loyal man. Handsome, dark skinned, built like a football quarterback, 6'5" tall with strong facial features; wide nose and thick full lips with dark brown eyes. He met the love of his life, my grandma Lilly Jane Truman, at a grocery store. She was a petite woman, 5'2", very fair skinned and could've passed for a white woman.

She had a pointed nose, paper-thin lips, curly wavy jet-black long hair and light green eyes. Beautiful. He told my father that when he first laid eyes on her, he went up to ask her where the flower section was. She didn't know so they went to find it together and when they got there, he bought her the biggest bouquet of flowers. From that day on, they were inseparable. He knew she would be his wife. My father told me my grandma was a seamstress. She learned how to sew at an early age; it became a hobby and she took it from there. Grandma would make dresses and hats for her church and for the women in the neighborhood. She was only eighteen but after my grandmother finished high school, with her parents' blessing they married within nine months. She was such a graceful woman that loved God, church and family.

My grandma from what I was told had some of the same characteristics as my mother. She introduced my grandpa to Jesus Christ and they were members in their church for years. She supported her husband and also had her own voice. They maintained a decent living but with all of the violence happening in Alabama they decide to move to a more remote location and the rest is history. They had one son; my dad. I was told that my grandpa would go into deep depression because of all of the racism from the people at his job as well as the neighborhood he lived in. Even though they moved things still kept happening and it didn't completely erase from his mind for a long time. My father said he would pray daily to be released from the haunting.

Years later he was delivered. My grandpa being that my father was his only son was really strict in his raising and he instilled in him: "To put God first! To take care of his self and to never let someone tell you; *you* can't be anything because of the color of your skin. Work hard and prove nothing to nobody." That was his motto and my father lived it to the fullest. He studied hard and excelled. He went to Tuskegee University and received his degree in criminal justice. My father met my mother in college. She was a psychologist major so they clicked right off. My mother Inez Ann Rossmore was raised by her widowed mother, Mary; her father Benjamin Rossmore was a carpenter and died of a heart attack when she was twelve. She was the oldest out of six children and she worked to put herself through college. She had to get a job at an early age to help her mom because she was a nurse and would work graveyard shifts. My mother helped raise her siblings.

She worked at a chocolate factory at fifteen years old. She started at packaging and worked her way up to management. She's had her share of racism at the job but still made it and now has her own private practice. My family lives in a modest middle-class brick home at 2710 Oak Hills Drive with five bedrooms and 3½ bathrooms. I went to Oak Hills Elementary School and Martin Luther King High School. I remember my father telling me a disturbing story about my grandpa when he was on the force about this one case he couldn't let go. It was about this elderly couple named Mr. and Mrs. Vaughn. Someone robbed and murdered them in their own home but there was no trace of evidence whatsoever. Back then they definitely didn't have the tools and research that they have now. The reason why it bothered my grandpa was because the couple use to watch my father as a child when my grandparents would go out for a night in the town or to play bingo. It was personal and a shock to the community.

The Vaughn's were so involved they would hold neighborhood watch meetings and have cookouts. They didn't have children so the kids they watched were like their own. Kids like my father; who would come as adults to show them *their* kids or just to visit. It was heartless. My grandpa promised himself he would find the people responsible for this heinous crime. All the way up to his dying day he would not stop; I see that in my father with everything he does. He is vehemently passionate and I've inherited the same trait; it's in the bloodline.

It took 25 years to find the suspect and my father told me throughout his whole college career, most of his adult life and five years before my grandpa died, he solved the case. He couldn't rest until the task was done. I didn't get the chance to meet my grandpa. He died before I was born but I could see his spirit in my dad. My grandma met me when I was eight months old and not long after she went on to be with the Lord as well. My grandpa actually helped my dad to get his experience in the field and I truly wished I could've witnessed it in person. I've seen pictures, heard stories and I'm grateful for that; it's not live and direct but I have my imagination. I want to be clear that my grandpa also solved multiple cases and gave his best to all of them even if they weren't as personal but it was this particular case that had his heart. My father told me being able to work with grandpa and actually solving a case was the most rewarding feeling he ever had next to marrying my mother and me coming into the world of course! I couldn't fathom the cases that my grandfather witnessed because there where so many hate crimes: not that today is any different cause it seems like history is repeating itself.

When I was three years old, my brother Ahmad Miles Rivers was born. I immediately became the over protective big sister; I felt that it was my duty to watch over him. I did and at times, a little bit too much to where my parents had to remind me that he was *their* child. He would call me 'Jo' because it was easier for him to say when he was a baby and he's called me that ever since; matter of fact he's the only one who does! He was such a cool baby; we had a bond before he uttered his first words. I use to play cops and robbers with him; I would sometimes force him to have a tea party with me every now and then.

When I turned six, I really started playing detective with him and all over the house. I would leave blood as ketchup around in the kitchen cabinets, on the stair railings and try to take a sample for DNA. I would leave fingerprints on the glass tables and try to find whose prints it was by interrogating *everyone* including my mom. I loved the board game Clue and my friends and I would do Clue reenactments. My father eventually broke down and finally took me to work with him; he worked at the very first police station in Fayetteville, which is the 7th district precinct on 42nd Street. I had a chance to meet everyone including the chief. They all loved how inquisitive I was and that I wanted to be a detective.

That following year when I turned seven, my father came home one evening very solemn. I can still see his face crystal clearly and it's been thirty something years ago. He came in the house and greeted my brother and I warmly as usual but even as a child I could sense he wasn't himself. He left us in the living room and went into the kitchen to greet my mother. I could over hear them talking; I pretended to play with my dolls on the living room floor. As he sat down and my mother brought him a cup of coffee, they sat in silence for a while. My mother was such a patient and kind woman. She could sense his spirit was troubled because that's the kind of connection they have. My father finally said, "We lost two of our men today." His voice calm but laced with devastation and disappointment. "Both of those officers were friends of mine. They have families like me and the guy is still out there!"

My mother gasped, "Oh no, Andrew!" As a child at the time I didn't understand why he was so distraught until it hit me that this isn't a game this *is* real life. One of those officers could've been my father and this man is on the run! Fayetteville was a small town around the time so everyone pretty much knew everybody, which was a good and bad thing. You couldn't get away with nothing; not even taking an apple off a tree without someone seeing you. So, for this man to vanish without a trace was serious. When I went to bed that night, I said my prayers and I asked God that maybe one day I could help my dad; like my father did with Grandpa.

My father is a semi big guy. He is medium height 5'8", slightly husky, peanut butter complexion, jet-black short hair, dimples, dark piercing brown eyes with a 1000-watt smile. Handsome indeed. He is a man of God, loyal, proud, respected and disliked. He's okay with it just as long as you don't cross our lawn without permission. Daddy protected us by any means necessary. My mother was a woman of God and she too was respected and loved. She had a slim frame, medium height for a woman about 5'5" with a brown sugar complexion, light brown doe eyes, medium length dark brown thick hair and a smile that could melt butter. Her whole disposition was warm, humble, regal and graceful. People loved my mother because she was true to who she was and what you see is what you get. She was strict about our homework and schooling, which was not to be played with. She made sure we went to Sunday school, church service and kept us involved in activities. She would say to my brother and I, "It's too easy to be a nothing!" She spoke her mind but with integrity and she was extremely intelligent. She was real in every aspect of the word. She loved people unlike my father who was a little bit of an introvert. He was the only child unlike my mother having to help raise her siblings. She grew up much more quickly from working at an early age and having to deal with people. No matter what both of my parents were doing, they would come to a common ground to be at every school parents' conferences even if it was just one of them. Football game, track meet, dance recital and science fair; whatever it was for both my brother and I they made it happen. My brother was popular in school, easygoing and he had a couple of friends but didn't get involved in any cliques.

He was a leader not a follower. I was also glad that he wasn't a jock but still loved sports and played all of them but football was his favorite. Ahmad loved science and wanted to be an engineer. Of course he would do annoying things like a little brother would do. He would hide my magnifying glass and chase my friends and I around with a scary mask sometime. I hate that mask! To this day he still has it and gets me every time! He hung around me a lot but when he turned ten it was over. I was glad that he was starting to become a guy and hold his own. He too has a brown sugar completion that resembles my mom except with chiseled facial features, pointy nose, perfect smile and hazel eyes; who knew where those came from! I was kind of jealous; a good jealous. He has light brown hair and is built like my dad. When he became a teenager, he stood at 6'0" passing Dad two inches! We would always tease that Ahmad could look down at him. I admired how my brother turned from a boy to a man literally overnight and became independent.

We weren't average children and our parents made sure of that. Segregation was still a factor in the 70s in Fayetteville but I'm glad my brother and I missed that part of history. Thank God for the civil rights movement. Our parents had us read an article they kept from the newspaper about the protest and marches from the students from Fayetteville State Teachers College (now Fayetteville State University) at the forefront; how it led to the end of whites-only service at restaurants and segregated seating in theaters. Blacks and women gained offices in huge numbers, from the late 1960s and on into the early 1980s. I also read about an army doctor just outside Fayetteville named Jeffery R. MacDonald. He murdered his pregnant wife and two daughters in their home in Fort Bragg, North Carolina in 1970! In high school I found out there was a book about this called *Fatal Vision*. I was flabbergasted because this grueling crime that was committed was in my home state!

In the 70s we were coming into our blackness with the Blaxploitation movies, music, hair and style. I missed that part being born toward the end; my parents were careful to let us watch certain movies even in the 80s but as we grew older, they let it slide. They let us watch Alex Haley's "Roots." My parents loved it and wanted us to realize how far how far we have come but still so far to go; that's why they embedded education in us. My father told Ahmad and I one night while we were in the living room studying.

"You have to work twice as hard and be twice as smart because of how society stereotyped us. You can do and be anything you want but you have to put in the work!" Those words soaked into my brain like a sponge and I believe it did in Ahmad's head too.

Q

My parents took us on road trips; I remember one road trip where we drove to Alabama to visit my dad's Aunt and Uncle Blanche and George Nickerson who lived on a farm ranch. Great Auntie Blanche was my grandpa's one and only younger sister. They lived in one of those white colonial plantation houses. Ahmad and I learned how to milk cows, rack hay, ride a horse; they even had mules and chickens. I would pick blackberries with my mom and we would bring them back to my great auntie so that she could show me how to make jam. Uncle George would ride the tractor with us on it; he would show us how the gears worked and let us pull the levers up and down. Everything was fresh and homemade; she even had her own vegetable garden with herbs and spices.

I've eaten some of the most succulent and delicious food I've ever had there; with all due respect to my mom's cooking which was also superb. The food wasn't bought in a store but raised with meticulous care and earthly soil. Ahmad and I would run all over their 40 acres of land; not too far from the house was a lake that was so serene. I would love to go and sit under the weeping willow trees and look at the water. Even then I knew what peace was; looking at all of Gods marvelous wonders made me appreciate my existence with every breath I took. We all would go swimming in the lake and Dad would dunk us in the water. Sometimes we would have teams, boys against girls, in a water football game. The stars shined so brightly at night there. My great auntie and uncle were quite the characters. My great auntie was a free-spirited woman she stood only 4'11", pleasantly plumped, fair skin, with a round, pretty face and short brown hair. She looked like a classic Cabbage Patch doll.

My great uncle was very tall about 6'3", slim statue but had a pot belly, midnight dark skin, with a head full of beautiful black hair that was pulled into a pony tail. He was very lively and fun; they complimented each other very well. They had one daughter her name was Dora but she died at three years old from pneumonia so they loved it when we all would come to visit. My great auntie has been trying since I can remember to get my father to move back to Alabama on the farm but he declines. I think that although my great auntie has her husband, she still would like to have my dad around plus with all of us not being close by she gets a little lonely. There are times where I would've loved to live there but I would get bored because there isn't any action on a farm; there's no one around but it's a blessing to be surrounded by nature. I live for adventure and I know that's what my dad lives for too!

I've had my share of boyfriends and I was grateful that my dad didn't have to hurt anyone. I had a boy who was a friend when I was a freshman in high school. He was very violent. I had no idea he had a Dr. Jekyll and Mr. Hyde split personality. His name was Sage. He was the center of attention because he could rap and during lunchtime his friends would have cyphers. He was nice looking; dark skin, with round, deep, brown eyes, 5'7" and a nice warm smile. He would call me 'Mysterious' 'cause we had a couple of classes together; one being a literature class and he knew I had a fascination with mystery stories. He had an arrogant demeanor but he was polite and asked me out on a date.

When we went to the movies, I gave him a peck kiss but he had other plans and tried to unbutton my blouse. I moved his hand away and he backed off for the rest of the date. When it was time to take me home, he went on a rampage about how he felt offended because I rejected his advances and he though I liked him. Before I could get a word out, he pulled off the road not even a block from my house and slapped me. In a complete daze at what just happened because it was so fast, I got out the car and told him, "My father is a cop!" I turned and started to run. With those words he followed and begged me not to say anything. I stopped running and said, "I would under one condition. I don't ever want to speak to you again. I forgive you but we have nothing; not even a friendship." He agreed and I never told my father till this very day.

Ahmad and I got baptized at Tabernacle Baptist Church when I was nine and he was six. God has and will always be first in our lives. When I was fifteen, I accepted Jesus Christ as my Lord and savior. I was at Bible study and I felt the Holy Spirit come over me; I started speaking in tongues. Ahmad and I were very young when we got baptized; we knew but we didn't quite understand what it meant to *be*

baptized. We went to Sunday school but it was still vivid in my mind. I had to get deeper with my knowledge of God and get to know Him for myself; it's imperative to be both baptized and saved. Here's a brief description; when you're baptized it symbolizes Jesus's death, burial and resurrection in water form. Your old self has died and now you're born again, living for the Lord. Being saved is a prayer acknowledging that you're a sinner. Believing that Christ died and rose again on the third day to save us from our sins. These two acts go hand in hand and being from a family that grew up in down south Baptist churches, I wouldn't have it any other way. We were blessed growing up and are *still* blessed and highly favored. In Jeremiah 29:11 it tells us that *The Lord has plans for us*. He has given me a gift to be able to use solely for His benefit. I could feel his leading and guidance in everything I do.

I knew what prayer was from the beginning. I was led by example when my father would tell me he would watch my grandpa praying. I too have seen *my* parents praying at the same time. Praying for peace, our nation, our neighborhoods, neighbors, schools, each other, and everyone. They believe in the power of prayer and can I tell you; prayer works! You know the saying the family that prays together stays together. It's 100% true and I'm a living testimony to it. My mother would go to early sunrise prayer and she would even pray late in the midnight hour; she's a prayer warrior. The scripture says in *James 5:16 The effectual fervent prayer of a righteous man availeth much.* I started to go with her to sunrise prayer and I'm such in awe of how my relationship with the Lord has progressed in doing so. I say this with love but it's not about being Baptist,

Christian, Catholic and any other religion because it's not religion; it's a relationship. There were times I felt I couldn't talk to my parents about something's; it may seem like I could but with the episode with Sage I had to go to God. He gave me peace and because I forgave him, I wasn't bitter. I was able to let it go without looking back.

My mother would say, "It's all in how you respond to the situation or circumstances." If I had responded to hitting him back, things really would've been catastrophic. I always try to remain calm when the storm comes or when misery shows up; I have a sixth sense. I think really quickly on my feet because things happen within a blink of an eye and I want to have impeccable timing to be able to handle whatever comes my way.

It's the mid-nineties now but the eighties were still going on strong. I'm sixteen and in my Janet Jackson mode. It seemed as if the wind shifted and everywhere I went I heard Heavy D and The Boyz, Rakim, MC Hammer. I still had my Run DMC tape. N.W.A. was making waves, R&B soul singers, Brandy, Monica, Mary J. Blige and Gospel music was getting more air play; Kirk Franklin was getting his STOMP on! My 1st cousin Ruth would come over my house sometimes and we would watch the movies that we loved; Krush Groove, Beat Street, Spike Lee's School Daze, House Party and everything in between. One moment Afros then Jerry curls and now box braids. James Brown to Big Daddy Kane, platforms to Adidas and drugs were really starting to affect the world.

In the 70s drugs were for fun as I saw in pictures and clips of Woodstock now it's a way of life. I remember a girl I had classes with named Stacy. She was extremely popular on the cheerleading squad and ran for class president in which she beat me by one lousy point! She looked to be most likely to succeed except for a major flaw: she hung out with the wrong crowd. My mother would say, "Everybody's not going to like you or become your friend." By the time senior year came she was strung out. She tried to hide it and she did but I could tell. I'm a very observant person and I don't open up at first; you have to smooth me out. I watch *everything* like my daddy says, "Someone is always watching!"

I became a part of BSU (Black Students Union). I wanted to befriend Stacy and invite her to some of our events because I could see where she was going. She was nice but didn't want to get to close to me, which I didn't understand *then* but I definitely know now. That was God because He needed to deal with her on His own but I made sure I prayed for her.

One afternoon after a track meet, one of our teammate's houses had gotten robbed and I was furious. I wanted to find out who did it; my dad told me to stay out of it but being hard headed I ended up asking my teammate some questions anyways. I had to get my Dragnet on with "Just the facts, ma'am!" I would watch old 60s shows too with my parents along with Perry Mason, Adam-12 and a host of others. It helped me out a whole lot with writing essays for class. My teammate Michelle told me there were tons of fingerprints and if I didn't love and respect my daddy so much I would've been there as fast as lighting! I was so upset at my father because she was my teammate and I wanted to help in some kind of way; I am nosy too but since that would be my career it would be a great way to start. He didn't want me to get hurt and I was still too young to get involved. I agree; it was just the stubbornness in me at the time.

My brother was laughing at me because he knew Dad wasn't going to allow it; my dad told me we would work together one day so I took his word for it. He had been stressed around that time because out of all the cases that he was able to solve his team still couldn't find the fugitive. They only had a composite sketch drawing of him by an eyewitness. I would see the flyers on the electric wood polls and see my dad's team walking around town with them to get some leads and no one came forth but the buglers were caught within ten hours! It was befuddling to me and certainly for him. As the years went by the case grew cold and while he was being persistent trying to find witness things were starting to get ruff at home. My mother had to tell him that he needed to let go and let God because he was driving himself crazy. We wouldn't see it because he knew how to hide it from us but not Mrs. Inez. He eventually retired from the case in regret.

Going to Homecoming dances and football games was so much fun! I spent the night at my girlfriend Elaine's house and lived life like a teenager. I met Elaine Shaw in our neighborhood. She moved around the corner from us. Her mother and father are divorced so she stayed with her mom during the week and the weekends with her dad. When I started walking to high school, I would see her. She had the cutest shoes on and when I stopped to ask her about them, we became friends from that day forth. We're six months apart. She's funny, stylish, nice and bossy. She doesn't care what anyone has to say about her. She's a rebel and definitely has my back as I have hers. Her skin looked like eggnog, yellow, rich and creamy. She is 5'3", petite, beautiful with brown straight shoulder length hair, and a modest smile.

We understand each other and since she is the only child, she latched onto me like a sister. Elaine and I didn't have to compete for guys and we weren't jealous of one another, which is a blessing. We had our share of arguments; don't get me wrong but nothing that would break our friendship apart.

I ended up having a boyfriend his name was Cory Kinsmen. He is God fearing, respectable, kind and handsome; with caramel skin, light brown piercing eyes, dynamic strong manly facial features, jet-black short wavy hair, athletic frame and about 6'0". He has a goofy sense of humor with a smile as bright as the sun. I met him at a church retreat I went on and to my surprise he lived in

Fayetteville but he went to Woodbridge High School. I met him the last night of the retreat. I didn't see him the whole time it was as if he appeared out of nowhere. For the last night there was a get together and when I walked in the door our eyes met and it started from there. I didn't go out on a date with him at first when we got back home until I was comfortable and he understood. We talked on the phone a lot. There were flaws; I'm talkative and stubborn and he was kind of stingy. I understood we were still getting to know one another and he would loosen up in time so it wasn't something that I couldn't deal with.

Some weeks went by and we went on our first date but not to a movie we went bowling and had a great time. He was a gentleman; he brought me flowers and opened doors. His grandmother raised him. Both of his parents had died in a plane crash. He is the second child out of three and he had to watch over his younger brother; how I watched after mines.

A couple of days after the date my parents felt it was time to talk to me about the birds and the bees. I was seventeen, a senior now and we have almost made out of the 90s; Dad was up first. Before I started running track, he and I would go jogging together for our bonding time. It was an early crisp Saturday morning and he was my alarm clock banging at the door as if he was a S.W.A.T. team coming to raid my room. We would go to Jesse Owens Park and jog for about 35 minutes and then we would go sit next to the pond and watch the little kids with their parents feed the ducks. My dad is a man of few words but when he does speak it's in your best interest to listen. As we sat in silence for a minute, he asked me a question, "Do you know anything about men?" he asked in a soft baritone voice.

I nodded yes and replied, "I know that you have to be straight up with them and let them know what you want."

"That's good to hear and that's one way but the key is to understand a guy. Men deal better with actions than words. He must be a Godly man and has accepted Jesus as his savior. Pay attention to his actions because it's going to say a lot about his character, interest and integrity. You have to know how he thinks. If you could get inside his head to make him think about you, you got him! Listen to him and hear him out when he needs your ear and he will do the same for you. Men are logical; so think logically not so much with your feelings as I know it's hard for you to do because that's in your nature but learn to separate the two. If he wants to call, he will. No need to hang around the phone. Chivalry is not dead so let him open the doors for you as I've already seen him do; so that's a point for you baby! Lastly, *BE YOURSELF* and never let him *DISRESPECT YOU!*" My dad was given me the top-secret *MAN* codes with this information. I felt confident and powerful; what better advice to get about men than from a real true man/hero: my father! I could tell that he was kind of nervous when he asked that question because of what my answer would be but since I gave a definite concrete answer, he felt okay to tell me the business. I hugged and kissed him and said sweetly with love, "Thank you, Daddy, I love you!"

Mom loved this place called Mr. Tea. She loved tea and kept beautiful sliver tea sets in our dining room and inside of the China cabinet. I absolutely love my mommy she is amazing and it was our time. She looked slim and dapper with her black *Breakfast at Tiffany's* inspired dress. It was simple, mid length and not to the floor. Her hair was in a neat bun; light make up with a hint of gold MAC lip-gloss. She loves jewelry; she had on a classic single white pearl necklace, earrings and bracelet set that her mother gave to her. I had on a black mid length sleeveless lace dress, my hair was in a bun too, and with my teardrop pearl earrings she got me for my sweet 16th birthday.

I wore a little bit of my MAC red lip-gloss that I bought a couple of days ago at the mall and a simple Tiffany charm bracelet with my initials MJR; it was a Christmas gift the same year I turned sixteen. When we were escorted to our seats outside to the patio, there was a beautiful, warm summer night breeze and it felt wonderful. We had an exquisite table for two with the sliver-wear glistening, the starched white tablecloths and crimson napkins with a gold ring around it, a white plate with the basic table settings; the knife and spoon on the right along with the water and beverage glass. The salad and dinner fork on the left. On our right side there was a flower wall divider for the inside tables. It looked like an upscale garden; whimsical and elegant at the same time. The tables were nicely spaced out so there could be privacy.

"How are you, baby?" my mother asked in her angelic voice.

"I'm well, Mom; I feel like I'm at a grown women tea party!"

We laughed; then she said, "I'm very happy to have this time with you and to have this women-to-women conversation. I want you to know that you can talk to me, Missy baby. You're growing to become an exceptional young lady and I want to make sure we maintain our relationship."

"Thank you so much, Mommy, you don't know how much that means to me to hear you say that," I said with tears starting to fall down my face. I thought to myself, '*I wanted to tell her what happened between Sage and I but I didn't want to ruin the flow of our evening. So, I'll let it go but I promise myself that if anything like that happens again I will.*' She held my hand and we started talking. The waiter was polite and took our orders; we ordered a pot of the ginger turmeric tea, which was delicious, and we both had the jumbo shrimp fettuccine with white marinara sauce with a side salad. I mainly wanted to sit back and listen because this is the woman of all women: *MY MOM.* It takes a strong woman to be with a man not just any man but *my father*; he was no joke and neither was she.

"What you do to get them is what you do to keep them but he must know the Lord and have a relationship with Him," was the first thing she said. "Always be a lady and say things in love, learn to speak softly and stay calm. Learn to listen and understand where he's coming from. Be

29

independent but don't forget to let a man know that he is needed as well. Respect one another. Learn to be friends first. Keep yourself up by dressing nice, smelling good and in shape when you can. When you start having children later on in life with your husband, do the best you can to not let yourself go. You smell quite nicely tonight. What's that perfume you're wearing?" my mom asked.

"It's Poison, Mom. Cory got it for me, remember?" I said shyly.

"Oh yes that's right! He is so sweet I can't wait to meet him! It looks like he already knows what he's doing!" my mom said and she laughed.

Laughing with her I said, "You will very soon."

She continued, "Compliment him sometimes; let him know that he is appreciated and loved but most of all *RESPECTED*. Lastly *BE YOURSELF*!" When we got home after the dinner, I felt a sense of contentment with my parents these past couple of days. The Lord opened up the opportunity for us to share, be closer and for me to not be afraid. I will still keep something's between God and myself. As long as He knows and I don't bind it here on earth and release it during prayer I'm okay with that. I admit I wasn't quite sure before if my parents were judgmental but I see there not. Will there be disagreements? Yes, but I will be respected for it. They want a relationship with me and that's all that matters. *In Matthew 7:7 it says to ask and it shall be given unto you*. If I'm not afraid to ask the Lord for things, why should I be of my earthly parents? The people God handpicked to raise and guide me as it says in *Proverbs 22:6 Train up a child up in way they should go and they would never depart from thee.* I couldn't have asked God to bless me with the greatest parents that ever lived. What was so interesting about my talks with them was that they were both on one accord; it's a sign of God and unity.

Then the day came where Cory meets my parents and I begged Daddy not to be mean and aloof. This was the first guy I brought to dinner with my family. Even though I went out with Sage, I didn't bring him to dinner 'cause you know the story! Mom made good 'ole southern fried chicken, corn on the cobb, mash potatoes and gravy, rolls with a garden-fresh salad. It smelled like heaven throughout the whole house. I was setting the table when, Ding Dong!

I heard the doorbell ring and I felt a dose of nerves come over me. My brother answered the door.

"Hey, man, what's up; I'm Ahmad," he said as he reached out his hand.

"Cory! What's up, man!" as he reached out his left hand with flowers in the right they engaged in a handshake. As they stood in the foyer Cory started small talk with my brother.

"Your sister talks a lot about you! I'm a football man myself. What's your favorite team?" Cory asked excitedly.

"The 49ers!" Ahmad answered with excitement.

"Oh yeah, we're going to be good friends!" Cory said. Just when their conversation started to spark my dad comes in from the garage. He walks in the foyer and with all the courage he could muster Cory reaches out his hand for my dad to shake.

"Hello, Mr. Rivers. I'm Cory. It's an honor to meet you and thank you for welcoming me in your home this evening," he said with a humble confident tone. My dad looked at him very keenly and with a nod and a slight smile he accepted his handshake. Ahmad had left the foyer as my dad was shaking Cory's hand and came into the kitchen to sneak a few peaks at the food.

I was in the kitchen as well but you know I'm nosy. I had walked to the doorway where I could see them both standing there. I heard my dad ask him, "Do you live around here?"

"Yes, sir, I live in Woodbridge with my grandma and my two brothers," Cory answered.

"Okay, I hear that you're a man of God, is that right?" my father asked.

"Yes, sir," Cory answered proudly. He took a deep breath and as he spoke the words flowed like a stream. "When my parents died and my siblings and I had to move in with my grandma, I was starting to feel lonely and upset with God. I was upset with Him for taking my parents but being introduced to the leading of the Holy Spirit by my grandma everything is working together. He sent me to my grandmother who is a powerful woman of God and with His grace, mercy, comfort and forgiveness He saved me. Before we didn't get to see her as much but now living with my grandma is the best thing that could've ever happened to us."

As my father listened in amazement, he soon recognized this young man has a purpose and he's all right with him! "Cory, come on in and have dinner with us," he said genuinely. Once the table was set Cory and my father walked into the formal dining room and my mother embraced him with a hug.

"I'm so happy to meet you! Cory, right? Welcome to our home," my mother, said smiling.

"Thank you, Mrs. Rivers, yes, it's Cory! I brought these for you."

As he gave my mother the flowers he said, "And it's a pleasure to meet you as well." My mom was very pleased with him as this simple act of kindness showed gratitude and respect. After grace was said and the food started to be passed around, we all were laughing and talking; it was nice. I'm glad it wasn't any awkward silences even though Cory is quiet and reserved he felt comfortable around my family because we're all connected to one source. *JESUS.*

Two weeks later I'm at a crossroads! I have to figure out what college I want to attend. I've always wanted to go to New York and I've applied to Columbia and NYU. However, I did apply to Tuskegee were both my parents went but I wanted to experience the big city. I've lived in this small town most of my life and I wanted to explore the world because it so much to see and to do. The last two colleges were Howard in Washington D.C and UCLA in Los Angeles, CA. I didn't tell my parents that I applied to major cities because they really have their hopes up for me to go to their alumni. I didn't even tell Cory yet; he's been applying to colleges close by because of his grandmother and younger brother. The only person I told was my bro.

"Do it! Go to New York, Jo. So I can come and visit ya!" Ahmad said as he was throwing his football in the air lying at the head of his bed. I was standing at the end of the bed in his room. "No, but for real go; you would fit perfectly there! I'm proud of you and I do wanna come and visit! I know the girls out there are *FIRE*!" Ahmad said.

"That's all you're worried about!" I said laughing at him.

"Thank you, bro! How am I going to break the news to Mom and Dad? That's my main concern. When I get an acceptance letter, *then* I would tell them. What do you think?" I asked him with a side smirk.

"That's perfect because how can they be upset that you are accepted to a college in one of the biggest cites in the world!" Ahmad said.

Walking home from school all I could think about was this is the day that the Lord has made and I'm going to rejoice and be glad in it but I'm a nervous wreck! To my calculations my acceptance letters should be arriving today and New York is up first. When I went to open the box, my hands were shaking. I saw three letters for me: New York City University (NYU), Columbia and Howard; Mom and Dad's mail = bills and miscellaneous. I didn't even wait to get in the house before I tore open the first letter: NYU; all I seen was: *We regret to inform you* and I crumbled it up. I hurried up and opened Columbia's letter and to my greatest achievement thus far until I become a detective, I was *ACCEPTED* to Columbia University in New York City. I opened up the last one and blessedly I was accepted at Howard too! With God and working my tail off I'm seeing the fruits of my labor; *now* I can tell them!

"NEW YORK CITY! What's wrong with Tuskegee?" my father asked in a loud alarming voice. I could tell he was nervous; I believe more nervous than I've ever heard or seen him. He's starting to understand that I'm growing up and want to officially leave the nest.

"Missy baby, that's wonderful but it's so far and that city is dangerous. Nevertheless I'm very proud of you and it's going to be hard for us but I'm behind you 100% baby!" my mother beamed with pride as she said those last words.

She is coming to terms a little bit better than Dad as I knew she would. He needed smoothing out; I'm his only daughter and first-born. It's tuff for him. "Well, it's hard for me, Missy. I just need time to process this! One minute you're following me around; the next thing I know you're going to New York. Not only for college but permanently; my little girl. I can't say I didn't see this coming but it's overwhelming!" His voice was starting to crack a little. I saw one tear fall to his cheek and I lost it.

On record I've only seen my dad cry one time when Ahmad was born and I held him in my arms for the first time. I ran to hug my father and he hugged me so tightly and said in my ear as he caressed my head. "I love you and I have to let you go. Dad is proud of you! You hear me?" he said in his most tender and sincere voice that I've ever heard. I nodded a yes and wept in his arms.

"I love you, Dad!" I said as I was crying. This was a turning point in both of our lives. My father will always see his little girl in me but as graduation approaches, I'm not only graduating and going to college; I'm growing into womanhood. All I did for the rest of my days leading up to prom and graduation was read and look up everything else that I might've missed about Columbia. I was so busy looking and reading at all the other schools in which I was applying to but now I could have undivided attention dedicated to Columbia and New York. When I would watch movies, I would get a glimpse of the city and it's out of sight!

"GIRLLL, what are you going to tell Cory?" Elaine asked as her voice sounded like a siren through the phone.

"I don't know but I have to tell him! There's no other way, so I have to prepare for the worse," I said in hesitation.

"I hear you but, Mist, you're going to New York! The fashion capitol of the world! I can't wait to come visit!" Elaine said.

"I know, and when I get my place, you'll be the first guest," I said.

"I'm going to miss you, but I won't be far since I'll be going to Philadelphia State. You know I couldn't let you be that far away from me!" Elaine said while laughing.

"I know and I'm glad. Thank you for being a sister friend to me and I'm happy that you're going to be close by. Now, pray for me about telling Cory!" I said laughing nervously.

"Will do! You got this, it's going to be alright!" Elaine said.

I had to take a break and now the hard part was the deciding factor on *when* I was going to tell Cory? I sat and thought for a while and I even went on a walk to do more contemplating. I love nature. I'm always outside or on my balcony bedroom window. I felt like Juliet waiting for my Romeo whenever I would sit out there. The view reminds me of my great auntie's farm looking out at God's land. This would be the times He and I would communicate other than going to bed and waking up to say my prayers. Being outside is my special prayer time and where the relationship with God comes in. I couldn't imagine my life without Him. I always first repent to Him to humble myself and recognize that I'm a sinner and then I start with whatever is in my heart. I also had to learn to listen to Him because He does speak!

I learn to watch because God works in mysterious ways. I've always loved that saying because He is unknown but yet known. You won't able to figure Him out; that's one case I could never solve and I love it! There would be times I wouldn't say a word. I didn't know what it was then but it's called mediation. I would close my eyes, take a deep breath, acknowledge my breathing and smell the sweet aroma of the honeysuckle flowers I was around. I would let the wind breeze rest upon my face, listen to the leaves rattle in the trees and hear the birds of the air whistling. I would take in all of my sense so I could appreciate the Lord and tell Jesus thank you for the air that I breathe and for whom He is. I take nothing for granted for tomorrow is not promised and life is but a vapor as the word tells us. I could feel the spirit come upon me and say, "*You will know when the way will be made for you, trust me.*"

❧

Senior Prom has arrived and I still haven't told Cory about my acceptance into Columbia. I believe when we go to the after-prom party that would be the perfect time. We haven't been sexually active and we're doing our best to maintain a clean relationship because of our beliefs. It's been hot and heavy at times. Kissing him is all I think about; it makes me feel good and his touch is very gentle. We try not to spend too much time alone because it will for sure lead into other things. We're human and the flesh is weak but we try to stay focused and lead not into temptation. I thank God for him because he could be doing other things and even with someone else but he is hanging in there with me or *us* I should say. That may all change once I leave for New York.

I decided to wear a lilac purple chiffon sweetheart neckline gown. The gown fitted at the waist, it had Swarovski crystals around the waistline. My mom had told the seamstress exactly what kind of bling she wanted on the dress. I had no idea what a Swarovski crystal was until I saw them when we picked up the dress and they looked like diamonds; I was elated. The gown flared out under the crystal waistline and it swayed like the wind with every step. I wished my grandma were alive so she could've made my dress nevertheless that's why I wanted the color lilac because it resembled her name "Lilly."

My mother let me wear her Swarovski crystal teardrop earrings along with the matching single tear drop necklace and a simple Swarovski crystal bracelet that made my French manicured nails shimmer. My hair was up in pin curls and it was beautiful; my hair is so thick that the curls looked like ribbons. I had my makeup done and it was flawless with a pinch of lilac eye shadow and nude lip-gloss; it was simple and stunning. When I turned around to look into the mirror after everything was complete, I almost didn't recognize myself and couldn't wait for everyone to see me! My grandma, Mary, was there; that's my mom's mom. She amazes me because at sixty-five years old she received her bachelor's degree in nursing. She's been a nurse since my mother was a child but she always wanted to go back to school and she did it!

That's where I get my drive and determination. My dad's friend Detective Dan Copper, my cousins; Ahmad and his friends, Bridge and Jontrae, and a couple of my mom's friends came to my champagne party. My mother had a small set up in the dining room for sparkling cider, tea, ordure's, fruit along with a veggie platter and finger sandwiches. She had a lilac tablecloth and napkins, lilac and sliver balloons at each end of the table, clear fancy plastic plates, with sliver plated plastic silverware for the kids but she broke out the china for everyone else. My mom is such a class act; anything she touches turns to perfection and this was no exception. My father was smiling from ear to ear; the air was filled with love, laughter and fun. When Cory arrived, he looked like he was ready to walk me down the aisle. I had to take a deep breath because he literally took it!

Cory was a king in his classic black and white tuxedo. He smelled so good and as always clean and neat. I had barely noticed his grandmother Mrs. Green; she looked so pretty. I met her when I went to her home a couple of days after the dinner date at my house. For her to be an elderly woman she was well kept; her skin was a flawless dark chocolate, her eyes were aged with wisdom; she reminded me of Cicely Tyson. Her nails were manicured and painted in lilac. Lastly, she had on a pretty white and lilac flower summer dress that buttoned up. I hugged and kissed her as she came by.

"You look wonderful, Misty," she said in her distinguished voice.

"Thank you, Mrs. Green, you look great yourself," I said coyly. His brothers were there too; Willie and Little Mickey. You could tell they were brothers because they all looked alike. Willie was taller and huskier in stature and super funny, Little Mickey was going to be the next heartthrob; even at eight he had green eyes, curly black hair and he would make the cutest facial features when I was around. He was shy and would turn red; so adorable. He would give his brothers the blues but when he saw me, he would run and hide. We took picture after picture outside in the backyard in our mini gazebo.

Then Cory took out the most beautiful white large gardenia corsage I'd ever seen and slipped it in on my wrist; it looked like the legendary blues singer Billie Holiday's gardenias. You would've thought the paparazzi were there with all of the pictures that were being taken. We decided to get a rental car for prom so that we could have transportation for the whole weekend since we were going to other parties. He rented a white 97 Ford Mustang Convertible and it was perfect. We gave everyone hugs and kisses and just before Cory closed the car door my dad said, "Don't make me come after you tonight, Cory!"

"No sir, she's in good hands. I promise!" Cory said. I turned to look at my dad and he winked at me and I blew a kiss. Prom was magical; we laughed and danced to my favorite song at the end of the night *Joy* by Blackstreet. Cory couldn't stop looking at me all night. Now comes the hard part and it's funny because I haven't even thought about it all day; so when I do tell him it won't sound rehearsed. When we arrived at my friend Liz's house, we found a comfortable spot in the den area of her home. Liz was chilled; she's the ultimate around the way girl, down to earth and kept it real. She is 'thickalicous' as she calls herself, has blonde streaks in her short bob hairstyle with brown Chinese shaped eyes and coco skin. She wears braces but she was still pretty. We had history class together and we clicked.

After we got settled into the den it was time; I could feel it! I took Cory's hand and looked him dead in his mesmerizing eyes and said, "These past few months have been so incredible and I really appreciate all that you have done for me; I truly care about you. I want you to know that I've been accepted to Columbia University in New York and I'm going to attend."

He turned his head and thought about it for a moment; turned back to me and said, "I'm happy for you and I know that this is something that you have always dreamed of. You have worked so hard to get this far. I don't want to stand in your way but you know what we have to do. We can't be together anymore; having a long-distance relationship is hard. I'm honestly saying I won't be able to deal with it. One thing is for certain; I love you, Misty." That was the first time he told me.

"I love you too, Cory." Tears of joy and pain rolled down my face. I had to get it together because this was our prom night. He didn't go to his so that we could have only one together and this was a special night. I expected this because he was right; I was going to be on the other side of the world. I would want him to live his life and not stand in his way either. It hurt but we have to set each other free; as my mother says, "If he comes back; he's yours!"

Class of "97."

It's been real but I can't wait to get out of here! I graduated on the deans' list and had perfect attendance all through high school. Graduation was bittersweet: all of the goodbye cries of my friends and teachers. My parents were beaming the whole time; my father was smiling so much it made my heart warm and subsided my hurt feelings. Although Cory and I weren't together he was able to attend the ceremony and I went to his too. We still have love, respect and friendship for each other no matter what.

As I packed the last box to my room, I took a minute to reflect on all the things that went on in here. The tea parties I had with my parents and Ahmad. My girlfriends would come for sleepovers, the tents Ahmad and I made with the sheets. The finger nail polish I spelled on the rug trying to do my toenails and when I got a whooping for it! I could go on and on about the only room I've ever known in my life. It was beautiful because my mom loves to decorate. She had a beautiful mini chandler hanging in the center. I love canopy beds so I have a white one that was against the wall next to my window with a balcony. Ahmad wants my room because of it; so I made a deal with him that he could move in but if I ever need to come home for good it's mine.

On my bed I have white, burnt orange and silver bedding that looks like I'm sleeping in the middle of autumn. Two silver nightstands with glass lamps on both sides of the bed. There is a silver vanity set across my room not far from my closet. Next to my closet is a desk where I do my work; on it is a little bookshelf where I keep some of the books that I'm reading for the month. I have a TV stand a few inches way. I had a couple of posters on the wall New Edition, Janet Jackson, Michael Jackson and LL Cool J. Some poems, quotes and Bible scriptures: Philippians 4:13 *I can do all things through Christ Jesus*. Langston Hughes, W.E.B Dubois, Zora Neal Hurston, Edgar Allen Poe and Aristotle.

All of that was now taken down and put inside this last box. My mom was walking by and peeked in; I could hear the door squeak open. I was standing at the end of the bed and felt her hands come around my neck. I can't say it enough my mom was a phenomenal woman she knew exactly when to make her presence known.

"Missy baby, you're going to be alright." As those words resonated in my ear I started crying. My dad maybe my heart but my mom is my rib.

"Cory and I broke up after prom and I've been numb not trying to feel the pain but it hurts," I said.

"I know how you feel; my mom continued. Your father and I had a break up before we got married. He wanted to see other people while we were in college in our sophomore year, I cried like a baby! She continued; my mom; *your* grandma told me that he would come back but for now keep your eyes on the Lord. It was ruff but I did! I surrendered to God and worked hard in my studies, lived my life and had fun. He came to a graduation party that one of my girlfriends was having and he told me, 'Letting you go was the biggest mistake of my life and I want to be with you and only you.' He got down on one knee and purposed to me!" This was my first time ever hearing this.

I don't know why I never asked my parents how my father proposed to my mom but here it is and this made me feel 100 times better! Not because of the hope that Cory and I may be together again one day but my mother revealed something about the both of them that I would've never known if I hadn't been in this situation. God reveals things when the time is right and we must trust Him and lean not unto or own understanding as it says in Proverbs 3:5. I hugged my mother so tight and she held me for a little while. I needed a mother's love and I thanked God for it. What a perfect send off for the next season in my life; I heard the spirit of the Lord say, '*You're ready!*'

Chapter 2
New York, New York

When I looked out of my window seat on the plane, I saw the ginormous buildings and yours truly the Statue of Liberty it all started to become real. As we finally landed onto the runway, I felt different; I'm officially going to be a New Yorker now. My whole way of living is going to take a dramatic turn. This is it; what I've been waiting for and it's becoming a reality. We landed at JFK airport and I was so happy that both of my parents were able to come because my dad was having scheduling conflicts. I'm glad it worked out or I was going to have to go down to the station myself and talk to the lieutenant! Not that it would've happened because my parents wouldn't allow it but I was going to talk to somebody; my daddy was coming! "Well, baby, here we are!" my mom said excitedly.

We were all excited because it's New York City! This would be an experience that we could all share together and that's what made it so special. "Missy, are you going to be able to handle this? It's so big!" my dad asked with concern.

"Yes, Daddy!" I said confidently, but I was so scared. I realized that I'm not going to have Ahmad and my parents around as much as I would like for them to be. Ahmad didn't come because he wanted to stick around the house.

He thinks he's slick because it's the first time he will have the house all to himself without Mom and Dad being in the same state.

He told me before we left, "I'm about to have the biggest party of the year! Wait and see!"

I told and warned him, "Be careful, lock the doors to Mom and Dad's room and mines as well! Put Mom's China and tea sets up and make sure Dad's things aren't lying around 'cause it's your butt if *anything,* even a penny, gets stolen!"

"Don't trip! I got this, Jo!" Ahmad said in a nonchalant tone. With that conversation in mind it made me want to cry 'cause I'm sure going to miss my little baby bro. He's so laid back and responsible; hopefully everything will be okay. We arrived a day early so we could have time to explore the city because the next two days were going to be busy with registration, meet and greets and unpacking. When we got in the taxi, all I could do was look at everything; I was in a trance.

"I don't see what's so good about this nasty place!" my dad said but when we turned to look at him, he couldn't keep his eyes off the window either. He was in his petty mood, as I was expecting. My mom and I were gleeful at the scenery; the taxi was driving on the Brooklyn Bridge and through the streets. "Baby, look at Sacks Fifth Avenue. Next time when I come to visit, we're going to go!"

"I would love it, Mom. We would be like those women on TV where we would have all those shopping bags in our hands walking around Times Square!" I said. Speaking of Times Square we drove right upon it!

"OH, MY GOODNESS! AHHHH!" Both my mom and I screamed at the same time with excitement! This was such a sublime moment for me and she felt it too. "WOW!" my dad said while gawking; even he had to give in to this moment. I could see the approval staring to flood his eyes. My father traveled to some states for work and for our family trips but New York he wasn't too pleased with. I think it's because he really didn't see what the big deal was; now with a new purpose he's looking at New York in a different way and it's starting to unfold as we're driving through the city.

"If you take a look on your left, you could see Central Park!" the cab driver said and it was the biggest park I'd ever seen. Surprisingly it was green and clean; New York is old and dirty but nevertheless it's special here! I was seeing so many different cultures, people of all walks of life and the air is filled with aphrodisiac vibes. I'm a loquacious person but I rarely said a word except, "LOOK OVER HERE!" "LOOK, MOM!" "LOOK DAD!" I was like a little kid in a candy store. We finally pulled up to the Beacon Hotel right in the heart of Times Square and it was very luxurious. A bellman opened our door with white gloves and a tailored black uniform. The hotel was a medium building not too big and it looked very classy; my parents have distinctive taste.

⚲

"WOW! This is beautiful; how did you guys find this hotel?" I asked as we walked in.

"Well, Missy, we thought that you deserve the best and we didn't want to come across the globe and not do it big for ya baby girl!" my dad said as my mom nodded in agreement. I was almost in tears as I looked around the lobby. There were beige marble floors, lush counter tops with gold trimming, Persian rugs, and chandeliers. Businessmen and women were walking up and down the halls. I saw a couple of families at the check in desk area as we were walking up to it. I turned to look at my parents, then the hallways; I was looking around attentively taking everything in.

While we were waiting in line I said, "Mom, Dad, I don't know what to say." I was trying not to cry because I wanted to be a big girl and show them that I could handle it; I let a few tears go and it was okay. I believe I've already shown them all what they needed to see or we wouldn't be here in the first place. The bellman took our luggage to the suite and I was amazed when he opened the door. Straight ahead I saw the biggest French window with a terrace overlooking most of Manhattan.

"AHHHHHH!" I screamed again with excitement! This was all starting to become too much; I was overwhelmed with joy that I forgot that my parents were leaving me here in a few days; I just enjoyed the moment and lived for today. There were two big comfy white king size beds; a big screen TV sitting on top of a cherry wood dresser that had six drawers with three on each side. The dresser extended to where there was a mini fridge filled with little bottles of water, wine, pop, liquor and enough space to put leftovers in. There was an olive-green sofa bed couch with some red, brown and mustard yellow pillows for decoration with a cherry wood table, which gave that section a living room feel to it. The bathroom was on the right side when you walked in from the front door. It was spacious and had beige marble floors too with glass shower doors and a separate tub right next to each other. There were two sinks with all of the hotel toiletries on each corner, nice starched white towels with the BH initials stitched in gold hanging on the shower armrest. Behind the door were two white robes, also with the same BH logo on the right side of them. The toilet was a few feet across from the sinks with its own door so you could have privacy. It was a clever touch I've never seen before in hotels until now. Most of them were open and you would have to close the main door, not in this case you could go while someone could come in; you still have to be warned but it works out. Directly across from the bathroom was a door with a decent size closet for our things and the carpet was vacuumed perfectly.

"Baby girl, what do you think?" my dad asked.

I'm a very opinionated person most of the time but not now I was still crying and speechless; all I could do is nod my head yes! I squeaked out, "It's the most beautiful thing I've ever seen."

"My Missy is so happy!" my dad said with approval. We went to dinner at Carbettea; it's the oldest restaurant in New York City since 1904 and the family still owns it! This place had my mother and I written all over it; French provincial chairs, chandeliers and candlesticks everywhere. It was an exquisite replica of a royal palace. I truly felt like a princess amongst my king and queen parents.

'Today is the day that the Lord has made and I'm going to rejoice and be glad in it!' I said out loud to myself. It's August 30, 1997 and I'm feeling good; ready to register into Columbia! I was once again cultured shocked by the people in line and I loved it! I can't wait it's going to be the best experience of my life. I was so happy that the registration lines weren't so bad! I was looking for them to be all around the school but blessedly they were in alphabetical order in one area. There was an Asian man waiting by my letter range: R-S. This may sound strange but I've never seen an Asian person, *in person* before so I was intrigued. His nametag said "Akio." He was about my height, slick black hair, and tan skin; tight eyes with a gummy smile. He was very polite and his English was great.

"Hello, welcome to Columbia. Can I have your name please?" Akio asked.

"Thank you! Rivers, Misty Rivers."

"Okay, let me see here," He said as he looked down the list.

"What does your name mean?" I asked him.

He looked up and smiled gently and said, "Bright boy!" He laughed as I did too!

"Oh, that's nice; I'm quite sure you are!" I said while still laughing.

"Thank you!" Akio said as he found and checked off my name.

"Alright…here is your information, Miss Rivers. The Columbia welcome packet inside is the map to the campus, your dormitory house, room number, your schedule, all of the events, activities and more classes that you may want to take next semester and up until you graduate. I'm quite sure that you will do well here, Miss Rivers," he said sincerely.

I laughed shyly and said, "I believe I will, thank you!" When I turned to walk away, I looked inside my packet and took the paper where my dorm room was and it said: The living-learning center. I read that it's the only all class integrated residential hall. My room number is 700. When my parents and I walked through the campus, it felt as if they were taking me to my first day of school; they stood very close by. I was starting to see their concern because there was so much going on; not bad things just interesting things. I've never been around so many different people it was a rainbow; delightful and refreshing. I told myself, '*I'm going to take advantage of this experience!*'

I see a lot of new comers coming in, paternities and sorority houses, some hippies, military men and women, football guys and the geniuses since I don't like to use the word nerd. "This is wonderful for you, Missy baby; you're going to learn way more here; meeting new people and traditions," my mom said enthusiastically.

"I'm glad you decided to come, Missy!" my dad noted. All I could do is nod and smile gloating on the fact that my parents are starting to see things from my side of the lens and it felt rewarding. We reached room 700 and when my dad opened the door my roommate was already there.

"Hi my name Etta Lyons! Is this your first year too?" Etta asked. She was Caucasian, red hair, blue eyes with freckles she reminded me of Pippy Longstocking. Don't act like you guys didn't read her when you were a kid 'cause I sure did! Pippy stood for independence and loyalty two of my most valuable traits.

"Hi, Etta. I'm Misty Rivers; these are my parents Mr. and Mrs. Rivers and yes, it is!" I answered.

"Cool! Nice to meet you all!" Etta said, as each one of us shook her hand.

"My folks left yesterday so, I'll be in the room," Etta said.

"Oh, that's too bad we didn't get the chance to meet them," my mother said.

"They'll be back to visit after the first semester and then maybe we all can have dinner together," Etta said excitedly.

"Sounds good!" my father said as we were dropping all of my things off.

"I'm from Boston, Massachusetts; where are you from?" Etta asked.

"Fayetteville, North Carolina," I answered. Etta had a Boston accent, which was interesting because I've never heard anyone talk like that. This was going to be fun she seemed nice; I could tell she kept to herself. She's personable and not afraid to have a conversation. Our room was a basic room with each side having a twin-size bed with the right bed to the wall and the left bed facing adjacent to the medium size closet on the left side. The closet door is behind the main door that we both had to share and mostly everything was on the left side of the room. There was a mini sink and a medicine cabinet above the sink and right next to it was a small desk; next to the desk was an average Jack and Jill bathroom that we would share with someone next door.

A medium size window above our beds and in between us a nightstand and blessedly there were three drawers attached to the sides of our beds. I got the bed with the wall so I could put up my poems and posters. Etta was cool with it as long as I gave her the nightstand drawer; that was a deal. As we were leaving from my dorm room, I felt really good to share space with a young lady of a different ethnicity especially Caucasian. Being born and raised in North Carolina that's not common. I had a revelation at that moment; I get the chance to break down a racial barrier. Knowing my parents never experienced sharing space with a white male or female; hopefully my bro will follow suite when he goes to college. He'll be graduating in a few years but I think he may go where my parents went to school.

"What do you think about your roommate?" my dad asked curiously as we walking down the hall.

"Well, Dad, I think she and I may get along just fine. She seems to be neat and negotiable," I said and started laughing.

"That's my Missy!" he said as he put his arm around me.

A day later I had to say goodbye to my parents and it was harder than what I thought it would be. I hugged them both so tightly I thought I was going to strangle my father!

"Ah, baby, we'll be back to see you! Now, pull yourself together, you hear me?" my mom said as she was fighting back her tears as well.

"Yes ma'am," I said with a little bit of strength in my voice, with tears in my eyes. "Missy, we gotta go now," as I heard a crack in my dad's voice.

"I love you both so much; I won't let you down," I said confidently.

"We know," my dad said calmly. We had prayer for traveling mercies and within minutes they got into the taxi and was gone. As I was waving bye the feeling became surreal and in color. This is where my life as I know it begins; there's no time to waste. I stood there for a moment. Alone, people walking all around me; everyday people and I were amongst them now. When I started walking back up to the school I became; *HOME SICK* quickly! I found an empty tree to sit under and I wept; I had to get it out now because it was sure enough going to come later. After about 15 minutes of crying I got up and started walking all over the campus and started praying. *"Lord God thank you for this opportunity that you have given me to be able to come to New York safe and sound with my parents; to have such wonderful parents and a roommate. Thank you, Lord, for blessing me with the gift of prayer to be able to speak to you about anything; giving me the wisdom to listen and be obedient to you. Thank you; Lord, for lifting up my head and being here every step of the way. Bless and protect the campus, the teachers and the city. With this prayer I ask in your son Jesus name; Amen."*

Mrs. Violet Cruz was no joke! What I love about college is that unlike high school you don't have to be here; the choice is yours. Mrs. Cruz was the toughest teacher in criminal justice; she was a no-nonsense woman born and bred in the islands of Belize. She came to America alone and raised her three sons; all of them went to college and are successful. She was passionate about teaching and only wanted to teach to those who wanted to learn. She knew the law back to front and would fail you before you could fix your lips to give an excuse; unless she felt it was worth listening too and even then, it better be good! I respected her. She was tall for a lady 5'7", medium frame, she had big hands and her hair was cut in a short hairstyle that resembled a curly fade for a woman. She had full lips, pug nose, dark brown eyes and her Belizean accent was so sharp it could cut you with glass.

"Misty gurl, yor doin good; keep up the good werk!" Mrs. Cruz said to me in class one day.

"Yes, ma'am, and thank you, Mrs. Cruz!" I said enthusiastically. If she gave you a compliment, you hit the jackpot!

I was always drawn to like the professors that were really strict; you could learn a lot from them and they pushed me the hardest. No, I'm not a teacher's pet; I take care of my business! My dad always told me, "That's how the world works; it's tough, challenging and it can chew you up and spit you out like a piece of old gum." Thankfully, I passed her class by the grace of God because she was a Goliath. Living in the city was defiantly the right decision although it can be a bit overwhelming at times. I loved all the diversity and any ethnicity you could name was here.

One Saturday morning I decided to jog though Central Park and to my surprise there was a young girl that was dressed up in what seemed to be a wedding gown accept it was powder blue with a halter top design. The bottom was shaped as a big flower bud; her hair was up in Shirley Temple curls with a princess tiara right in the center. Her friends were also wearing powder blue but their dresses weren't as extreme as hers and a couple of guys who were dressed in tuxedos were coming together taking pictures.

I thought I was actually witnessing a wedding; everyone looked to be of Hispanic descent. I walked over to the photographer and asked him what was going on. He said with good English, "It's a Quinceanera!" he said.

"What's that?" I asked. "I've never seen or heard of anything like this!"

"It's a coming of age for a girl when she turns fifteen; it's our way of saying she is grown," he said.

"GROWN!" I said, with a, 'what you talking 'bout Willis' voice! "Can she pay her own bills; can she even drive yet? I couldn't believe it! I sure wish my family was here to see this they would think this is absolutely insane." However, I remembered something; everyone has their own traditions. Everyone isn't the same and that's what makes the world go round. God made everyone in His own image. No one is alike; even a twin has his or her own set of fingerprints!

As I walked away and saw all of her family, how everyone was so happy and excited about this time I understood that although she's only fifteen it's not her age it's about her character; her stepping into women hood. This is how they celebrate it! I made a mental note to look up what a Quinceanera really means and why the Hispanic decent celebrates it; it looks amazing! I thought to myself,

'I guess that's why we have a sweet sixteen celebration; I sure did! I'm going to have a talk with my mom when I get to the dorm!'

I couldn't wait to finally go see the hit Broadway show 'CHICAGO'; along with that my parents surprised me with a visit! My roommate kept it a secret from me and I should've known something was up because my mom wanted to speak to her; not that they don't ask about her it was still odd. I finally made it to my senior year class of "2001!" I was so exhausted and also overjoyed because I was near the end of my college life; unless I go back for undergrad school but in this case, I'm finished for now. I've developed a relationship with a guy named Ocean Gains. I loved his name and he was amazing. God fearing, with a smooth brownie complexion, a small gap in his teeth, baldhead, with a nicely groomed thick beard and dark brown eyes. He has a slim athletic body, medium height around 5'8"; with an infectious laugh and a sweet candy-coated smile. He's cool, calm and relaxed and his name suits him to the tee.

I met Ocean the last semester of my junior year when I was jogging in Central Park. I saw him jogging pass my way and he too stopped to look at the young girl that was taking pictures for her Quinceanera. As I started to walk away, he came by and tapped me on my shoulder and when I turned around and made eye contact with him that was it! He also attended Columbia and graduated last year with a degree in Art History; he wants to have his own art gallery here in

New York and now he's studying to get his masters at NYU. Our relationship is not romantic; he understands that I want to wait until marriage however we do hold hands, we have cuddled and a kiss here and there but we both know what time it is.

Ocean is very thoughtful and the ultimate gentleman. He's authentic and that's what I respect about him; there are no mask on. He comes from a single parent home; his father Oscar and mother Joanne Gains divorced when he was five. He still has a very close relationship with his mother even though he chose to stay with his father. He is his father's only child and remained a bachelor. His mother remarried; had two children that are his little sisters, Emma and Beth, they are fifteen and twelve. He will be my date and gets the chance to meet my parents tonight as we go for dinner and the play. I've been dying to see 'CHICAGO' and the night has finally arrived. I couldn't wait till dinner was over it was nice but I was ready to go. My mother and father were really accepting of Ocean because he was a manly man. My father respects men who know God and where they want to go in life; he's about results because faith without works is dead. My dad respected Ocean; my mother fell right in line.

The performance left me in amazement. All of the intricate details with the set design, the lighting was spectacular, the choreography had me awestruck, the costumes made me giddy, the acting was superb and the plot was right up my alley; Murder. It was funny and weird because all the main ladies were killing their husbands to stay in the limelight; it made the show hilarious but the story was touching. Someone did get hurt not physically but mentally and that's all I'm going to say in case you ever want to see it; I don't want to ruin it for you!

I have two weeks left until graduation and I did it! With God on my side He helped me; He gets all of the glory! There were times when I wanted to throw my books and desk out of the window; the frustration, confusion with so many advanced subjects, the different teaching techniques from the professors was starting to stress me out but God was there. He never fails. As I walked around the campus, I felt *way* different than I did when I started because I've grown so much; not just in my life but in my spiritual life as well. My prayer life is on another level; I have a prayer time and an actual closet that I go into.

I've learned to mediate more on the scriptures especially the scripture: Psalms 46:10 *Be still and know that I am God.* I'm trying to have that in my spirit to know to let go and let Him be who He is and not try to stand in the way. I always feel like I have to step in and help God but I'm only hindering myself in the end. There has been plenty of times we're I've said to myself, '*WOW, see, Misty, if you would've let God do His thing, I wouldn't even be in this situation.*' But that's the wonder of having Jesus as our savior because He is here to save us. I will be twenty years old when I graduate due to my birthday being in September; I won't be 21 till later in the year but I'm grateful of how far I've come. His grace has helped me to be in a place of contentment with where my life is heading. I plan on staying in New York. I've been apartment hunting and Ocean has asked me to live with him; I respectfully declined. I believe we will end up being sexual and the talk about marriage will be out the door. Not saying marriage is the end all to be all but I want to do the right thing. I want to have my own place and he will have his. I don't know how we will work so with much prayer and consideration I decided to set Ocean free. I want to grow some more and if it's meant to be it will be; I'm putting it in God's hands.

I got a job at the Waldorf Astoria Hotel as the front desk concierge; it's something until I get accepted into the police academy. I'm going to be a cop in one of the most dangerous cites in the world; that's a tough pill to swallow but it will happen. I've asked the Lord to prepare me mentally because the world is different than sitting in a classroom that's for sure! I'm going to be dealing with scum criminals literally at the bottom of the barrel. My dad has been stressing because he knows it's only a matter of time for me to enter into *his* world; no matter how many times I have said "Daddy, it's going to be okay", he still gets queasy every time I bring it up.

Three days before graduation I got a call from my brother. "Hey, Jo, how are you?" His voice sounded sad.

"I'm good, bro, what's up?" I said curiously.

He hesitated then said, "Grandma Mary is sick—" he took a deep breath—"really sick, Jo," Ahmad said.

I held the phone for a min to catch my breath.

"Jo, are you there?" Ahmad asked.

"Ah…yeah," I said with a shaky voice. "What's wrong with her?" I asked hastily.

"Mom said her kidneys are bad and she may not have much longer to live; they're giving her one month," Ahmad said.

I couldn't say anything at all; I thought to myself, '*How long has she been sick and how come I'm finding out now? We talk most of the time and she hasn't said anything. She's been keeping this from me; she knew I would take it hard.*'

"Where are Mom and Dad?" I asked abruptly.

"They're on their way to see you and I will be leaving later on tonight because I have to do a few things before I come. I wanted to tell you because Mom and Dad didn't know when the time would've been right. So, I told you. That way you knew why Grandma wasn't going to be able to make your graduation. Don't be upset with them; Mom isn't taking it well; she is hiding it to save face but I know she's hurting. Grandma has been sick for months but it starting to get more severe now." Ahmad said. I thought to myself, '*God bless his heart for telling me.*' I took a deep breath and let out a weak "Okay." I couldn't even be mad at any of it because my parents didn't want to add on the extra stress and wanted me to focus on my studies.

"I love you, bro. Thank you and I'm sorry if I kind of snapped at you. I can't wait to see you!" I said to my brother with love and sadness.

"Don't trip, Jo, it's all good. I love you and can't wait to see you too!" he said happily. After I hung up, I was sitting there thinking, '*I haven't seen my bro in a year and how grown he sounded; such a man and very level headed about the whole situation. I'm so proud of him.*' He's now a college man; he goes to UCLA in California. My stomach started to hurt after what he told me had ultimately resonated in my mind. My grandma is dying. It was two extremes; what is going to be the happiest day of my life turned into the saddest.

"Missy, we wanted to tell you but there wasn't a right time for us to do so," my dad said as he was standing over me; I was sitting in the chair by the desk of their hotel room. I was looking directly at my mom and she was crying; so was I.

"I know, Daddy, it's okay; I'm not upset," I said calmly. As I walked over to my mom and hugged her really tight, she started crying even harder along with me; it was my turn to console her and I was honored to be there to do so. As she lifted up her head, wiped her nose with a Kleenex and collected herself she said peacefully, "We'll get through this baby; I don't like seeing my mother suffer; she will endure and it's the Lords will whatever the outcome is. I'm just going to miss her," my mother said as more tears fell from her eyes.

"I know, me too," I said calmly. I couldn't sleep that night; even when I'm stressed, I could still sleep but the thought that someone who is close to me doesn't have much time to live made me think. I knew I had to get prepared but no matter how much preparing you do, it's still going to hurt and badly. So, I go to the very person that can tame my thoughts and give me the peace that surpasses all understanding. *JESUS*. I got out of bed and on my knees; my favorite place to be and started praying:

"Lord Jesus, forgive me for all my sins; seen and unseen. I come to you to lay down my burdens and to ask for peace for my family for this storm we are about to endure. I thank you for blessing me to have had and enjoyed my grandma. You have allowed her to have my mother and in turn for her to give me life. I thank you Jesus and I'm eternally grateful for your loving kindness and tender mercies. Thank you for her life and helping her to overcome obstacles, to achieve life goals and making her dreams come true. I know she is in good hands and I love you, Jesus. Thank God, in Jesus's name I pray Amen."

Chapter 3
On My Own

"Hi, Grandma, how are you?" I tried to muster enough strength in my voice to speak to her. It was graduation morning and although everyone who I loved was there I still felt a piece of my heart was missing. My grandma has worked so hard for so long; she's one of the most resilient and strongest women that I know. Before we left the hotel, I had to have my moment with her.

"Hi, sweetie, sorry Grandma couldn't be there but you know I'm there in spirit. You just don't know how proud I am. Grandma's going to be alright; you don't worry about a thing. Today is your day and you take that well deserved walk to receive your degree; you earned it!"

Warm tears flowed down my face; my grandma was dying but she sounded amazing. Not even dying could take away the joy she felt in her spirit on this special day. "Grandma loves you; you're going to be a fine detective. I will see you in a couple of days when you get here!"

"Yes, ma'am. I love you so much, Grandma," I said with my quivering voice. As I hung up the phone, I felt I had been given the seal of approval; I could face my graduation with confidence. I'm the Class of "2001!" It was a beautiful June summer day as if the windows of heaven opened up and poured me out a blessing. I could feel a fresh anointing in my soul glowing from the inside out. Another part of my life was coming to a close and a new chapter begins.

We finally landed in North Carolina days after my graduation. I couldn't wait to see my grandma's face. She was all I could think about during the whole flight and also for me to find an apartment, which my parents offered to help with. After my visit here we're off to Hawaii; a gift from my parents and my apartment too. The wait list is long to get into the academy and I have to start from the bottom, go through with being an actual police officer first before I can make detective. My parents offered to pay one year's rent for me until I get on my feet since my job at the Waldorf was temporary.

I thank God for such amazing and frugal parents. They have been saving since I started college and I was blown away by their generosity. The town seems so much smaller since I've been away for a while; the more things change; the more things stay the same. I feel like I've outgrown my hometown but whenever I come back, I'm eight years old again! I guess that feeling won't ever go away because this is my first love; always and forever my home. My heart started to hurt once we reached my grandma's house. I didn't know what to expect and how I was going to react; I kept saying to myself, '*Be strong; you got this!*' I was so happy the whole family was together again it gave me an extra push. When we got out the car, my dad came around me and put his arm over my shoulder for a quick hug; he grabbed my mother's hand as I walked up in front of them.

I was the only one who hasn't seen her; I asked everyone how she looked but they wanted me to have my own opinion; I respected that. They wanted me to keep a positive image of her in my mind and I love them all the more for it. As I walked into the house, I could still smell the fresh cedar in her home. Everything was in its original state; not even a hairpin was misplaced. Her home looked like a museum but there was a warm homely feel to it. She wasn't in the living room sitting in her favorite chair she was upstairs and before I started to go up, I heard a voice; one that I would never forget shouting in a happy and excited tone, "MISSY! GET UP HERE! AWWW! MY BABY IS HERE!" You would've thought I was Flo Jo the way I ran up those stairs; her bedroom door was open and she was sitting in her chair by the window; it looked as if she was reading. That's one thing I loved about my grandma she always had a book! I was a little shocked at first; she had lost a lot of weight but was relieved she didn't look like a walking corpse; it wasn't as bad as I prepared myself for. I know were not meant to be here forever but it's hard to say goodbye. We laughed and talked; I sat up under her; it felt good. I stayed for two days helping her with chores around the house. This moment brought so much joy because I knew time was short with my grandma, however, we still savored the moments and made them the best we could.

September 11, 2001

A couple of months after I graduated College only God knew that this day would change the whole world forever. I was able to live at the dorm for the rest of the school year; hopefully by the holidays I would be in my new apartment. I went to dance class that morning; I take classes sometimes to stay in shape. I'm not a ballerina but I'm pretty good. I take modern and jazz dance; quiet as kept after seeing the Broadway performance of Chicago I was bit by the dancing bug; you couldn't tell me I wasn't Velma Kelly! I always have fun with everyone in the class. My teacher; Mr. Dynamite is a fantastic dancer with explosive energy and has traveled all over the world. He's tall 6'5", dark skinned with shoulder length dreadlocks, wide brown eyes, slanted nose and a cute smile. We were all having a good time laughing and talking after class when one of the guys from another class came in; he could barely speak and by his body language he was so distraught.

"TH-TH-THERE IS A TERRORIST ATTACK!" he said while stuttering and shouting!

"WHAT—" I covered my mouth in disbelief of what he was saying. My friend Detrick and I started running out the class. Detrick is so talented, funny and he felt like a cousin from back home. We immediately clicked when I started taking the class. He's about 5'4", brown-skinned, boyishly handsome with a great smile. The receptionist didn't want us to take the elevator so we all started running down the stairs still not aware of what's going on. Once we opened the door to outside it was reminiscent of the movie Independence Day but this wasn't a movie. Everyone was running around in chaos.

Detrick and I looked at each other wondering what was happening because we hadn't seen anything yet.

"We need to find out what's going on, this is crazy!" Detrick said in an alarming tone.

"Right, let's try to find out!" After I said that I saw some of our classmates looking at a TV through a cafe window. When we walked up to see what they were watching, I saw the second plane crash into the other building!

"OH, MY GODD!" I screamed! Detrick and I started running! As I ran past the Lincoln center my phone-ranged; it's Ahmad screaming my name!

"JO! JO! OH, THANK GOD, I GOT YOU! ARE YOU OKAY?"

"YEAH, BRO!" I said hollering, running and panting.

"I'M GOOD, BRO! LET MOM AND DAD KNOW I'M OKAY! I'll CALL U ONCE I GET TO MY DORM. LOVE YOU!"

"OKAY! LOVE YOU TOO, JO!" After he hung up, I couldn't call anyone; the lines were busy for hours. I was happy I was able to talk to my bro. Once I got back to the campus everyone was panicking and running around not knowing what to do. I stood outside and waited like everyone else. My phone line had opened up much quicker because my line is from North Carolina. A lot of people wanted to use my phone to call their loved ones so I let a few use it. I did the best I could to help and I'm glad I was able too.

Detrick stayed with me for a little while and it was nice to have him around. He eventually left to go home; everyone was still outside the whole time including myself.

Three hours later I was talking to my parents and I had them on speakerphone.

"MISSY! YOU'RE COMING BACK HOME!" my dad said with anger and fear in his voice. This is the first time I ever heard him this way and he had every right to be upset.

"DAD, NO!" I caught myself; I didn't want to raise my voice. "Dad, no! I can't come back right now!" I said with reason and calmness.

"I know, baby girl; I need to calm down. I'm sorry it's not your fault and I can't take this! I can't do anything to help you; you're too far!" my dad said his voice was trembling. My heart was pacing the whole day and by hearing my father this way; feeling vulnerable it broke my heart. My mom came in; she was a nervous wreck too.

"Missy! Your father is right you should come home once this clears up!"

"I can't even imagine the families, the people, the first responders; God help them! We need a prayer vigil for everyone; all of us!" my mom said with compassion.

"You're right, Mom. We do and we will but I want to stay. I know I'm supposed to be here and I know this is an unfortunate event but God will continue to protect me."

"You're right, baby, and we know you have to live your own life; but you're still *our child* and we just want you to be okay. We love you; call us in the morning and try to get some rest. Go back to your room; we know it's hard right now but go inside," my mom said as she started to calm down.

"I love you, baby girl; talk to you tomorrow," as my dad chimed in; his voice sounded relieved.

"I love you both so much and I'm going right now!" By the time I got to the room I was exhausted. I didn't realize it before because of the adrenaline rush; I could collapse on the floor but I didn't. My roommate moved out so I was there by myself. I managed to turn the TV on and go get in the shower. As I continued to watch the attack on the news, I still couldn't believe what I witnessed. My heart bleeds for all of those innocent people, their lives and families. It's hard for people to believe that there is a God and why horrific things happen; they have every right to feel that way but the argument of *why* this would happen is in the Bible. Wars and attacks have been going on since the beginning of time by the *PEOPLE* not God. All for power, greed and evil in my humble opinion. What happened then happens now and unfortunately innocent blood is spilled. As it says in John 10:10 *The enemy seeks to kill, steal and destroy.* The saving grace through all of this is that the Lord didn't allow the attack to hit the building where my class was which ten blocks away!

The sky was looming in brown fog for days after the attacks. The air was filled with debris, smoke, and ash; I'm surprised we were all able to breathe. The city was in shambles as if it were Pearl Harbor all over again. The Lord shifted the atmosphere. New York is a rat race full of people running around like chickens with their heads cut off. Go, go, and go. Busy, busy, busy; now everyone has slowed down a tad. All I could do was pray for the world; it's sad that this had to happen in order for us to help one another.

To let our families and friends know that we love them. Jesus gave us a commandment to love one another and it's the hardest commandment to abide by. I really had to dig deep and ask myself a lot of questions. *"Love has no color, race or creed. Love is an action not a feeling. Where was the love in this?"* I was feeling really discouraged and the only scripture I could think of to help me was *Proverbs 3:5 Trust in the Lord with all thine heart; and lean not to your own understanding.* This scripture is embedded in my soul to give me peace and to stay in my spiritual realm. It's not for me to understand. My job is to show love the way Jesus did the best way I can. God has the whole world in His hands and He's got all of those people too. It's unfortunate how it had to happen but God's got 'em.

My 21st birthday came around and the mood was different. Some of those people won't ever get the chance to celebrate their birthdays again. I dedicated my birthday to the people, the first responders and health care workers. I went and volunteered at a couple of shelter's by serving food, packing lunches, organizing the donation center for clothes, shoes and furniture. I became a member for one of the shelters called The Good Shepard so I could continue volunteering on a regular basis. I went and spoke to a couple of first responders who survived the 9/11 attacks and helped pull some of the people out of the wreckage. One officer in particular, his name was Officer Thomas, was at one of the shelters I was working at. I had a chance to speak with him and asked if he was a part of the 9/11 call to duty; he said yes and was suffering from PTSD; he told me this, "I feel this way because of what I had seen and me dealing with PTSD is nothing compared to what those families of the lost loved ones are feeling. We even lost some of our men and women as well but I will be okay in time and I hope they will too. I don't regret anything and I'm honored to have helped rescue a lot of people. This is a storm that the Good Lord will walk all of us through and I'm victorious not a victim!"

I looked at him with a huge amount of admiration and respect. I gave him a hug and said to him, "Officer Thomas, thank you for your loyalty and love for the people and your faith in our Lord Jesus Christ; knowing that you'll be alright." As I walked away, I thought to myself, '*One day I will be a part of the police force. If I was an officer around that time, I would've been there to help; I may have even lost my life in doing so.*' The Lord says as I mentioned before about love being the greatest commandment; but in John 15: 12–13. The Lord says: *This is my commandment; That ye love one another, as I have loved you. Greater love hath no man than this, that a man lay down his life for his friends.*

As this year was already tragic my grandma passed away in her sleep a day before thanksgiving. It was the darkest time in my life but the peace I felt within was nothing but Jesus. The word tells us in *Isaiah 26:3, If you keep your mind stayed on Him; He will give you perfect peace.* It seemed that her spirit came right inside of me; I could feel her as God said He is with us and you can definitely feel His presents. My mom is doing okay; she has her moments. Everyone is mourning; you feel as if something inside you has died. We'll be okay and move on but we will mourn in waves.

Looking at the drab walls in my apartment in New York I couldn't believe it was actually mines. My parents helped me find a nice studio flat in Harlem on 125th Street. As soon as you open the door, there is a window straight ahead; you could see a view of the building across the street. I could see some of the tenants through their windows but since my building is a far distance away, I wouldn't be invading their privacy. The living room area is by the window, to the left was a mini full kitchen, no dishwasher of course; it's fine since it's only me anyways and there was just enough closet space. I would have to limit buying extra things since my storage area is limited. Through the kitchen was a small yet compactable bathroom with a bath/shower; a bonus! I'm grateful that the Lord found me a safe and clean place to be. It's insanely busy on this street not too far from Malcolm X Blvd.

Almost every corner had a braid shop. There is so much culture and texture oozing the streets; I loved every inch. Some food restaurants, clothing shops, music stores, it was a new generational version of the Harlem Renaissance; it wasn't as polished but the vibe was in the air. I didn't live far from the world-famous Apollo Theater. The feeling you get from living next to a piece of history was priceless and worth the seven flights of stairs to walk up to my place. I couldn't have felt more liberated but also scared out of my mind. I didn't want to show it to my parents; any sniff of fear and they would've moved in with me! "I think I'm going to paint the walls so that I can have some light. What do you think, Mom?"

My mom responded in her ecstatic voice, "That sounds good, Missy. I'm ready to decorate!" My parents stayed around for two weeks to help me get my place in order. We bought dishes, sliver wear and I got a beautiful rug to lie over the old, but in good condition, hardwood floor. A divider so I could separate my living room and bedroom. I got a pullout loveseat couch so when I have visitors; they have a place to sleep. I set it against the window its mint green with two identical pillows in lilac purple, a dose of mint green and white blended in. A full bed bedroom set with a mini dresser and mirror. The most important thing it needs now is the anointing oil over every doorpost in the house. With my parents' prayers it's a brand-new place; full of God's love, protection, warmth and coziness. I can let out a sigh of relief knowing I'm officially on my own.

"Mist girl, this is sooo cute! I love your place and how you have it all set up; it's really nice," Elaine said as she was sitting on my loveseat while putting her feet up on my famous coffee table. When I told her I had my place, she couldn't wait to get out here!

"Ummmm excuse me this is not your mom's house! I'm going to need for you to get your feet off my coffee table!" I said as I was laughing.

"Oh yeah, girl. I'm sorry. You're right but it sure is nice in here! I'm proud of you; you doing it, girl!" Elaine said full of excitement.

"I'm trying to, I'm really appreciative of my parents because not too many people have the help you know; I thank God! I don't take anything for granted," I said humbly.

"I know that's right and having a stable support system is a must; without that it's much harder. Not saying you can't achieve anything if you don't have the support because you can. I've seen people who didn't and were able to make it in life. It just helps to know someone cares!" Elaine said genuinely.

"Amen! I couldn't agree with you more!"

The next morning Elaine and I went church hunting. We took the number 9 train to 137th street and walked up and down Harlem to find my new church home. Most of the churches were nice but if I don't get the Holy Spirit feeling it's not the one.

"MIST! I'm getting tired of walking; I'm not in a marathon! I understand that you don't want any church but we may have to call it a day!" Elaine said with a bit of irritation in her voice.

"Okay…okay I know it's coming soon just a couple more! I'm glad you're here with me to do this. I would've done it alone if I had too but you came at the right time so I jumped on it; hang in their pleaseeee! I love you!" I said smiling and lovingly hugging her.

"Alright! For real two more that's it! I love you too!" Elaine said. I knew once we stopped into the last church that this was the one. When I walked in, I could picture my grandma sitting in the pew. The church is called Revolution Church of God In Christ; with Pastor Jeremiah Hughes Sr. and first lady Ava Hughes. It was in the middle of service and semi packed but we managed to get a good seat in the center. I love the smell of an old school church; it's something that I can't explain. As I sat there listening to the sermon, I could feel a fire rising up inside of me. When the choir soloist started to sing my grandma's favorite song *"There's a place In heaven!"* I immediately burst into tears. The spirit fell all over me. This was my church! After I calmed down and settled into the sermon, I heard the still small voice of the Lord say, *'Welcome home!'*

Chapter 4
New Territory

"NO!" and "NO!" No should've been my last name; that's all I heard from almost all of the letters from the academy. I've been in Harlem for six months! I've had jobs; waitressing and retail to get by but they kept declining my application and I'm appalled. I didn't use the fact that my father is a Homicide Detective to get in; I wanted to do it in my own merit but it's really starting to look like I may have to 'cause a sista is struggling! I don't want to ask my parents for anything I'm doing fine however, if I can't get into the academy then I'm going to have to go back home and apply there. That's the last resort! I will not under any circumstance give up 'cause the Lord brought me too far to leave me.

I've been working two jobs and it's been okay; I don't mind working hard because you have to do what you have to do. As I came home from a long day, I was glad that I didn't have to work both jobs tomorrow so I could regroup, get my thoughts together and affairs in order. I walked in my building and checked the mail but I was too tired to open it; I walked up the seven flights of stairs and finally opened the door to my place. I dropped the mail on my little table I have at the front door. I got ready to take a nice hot bath and relax to some Jazz music; I feel asleep in the tub and when I woke up the water was cold as Alaska. I got myself out, dressed and collapsed on the bed. I looked over and saw this letter sitting up on my little table as if it was waiting for me to read. I know it was nothing but the Lord giving me the strength because usually once I'm on the bed; I'm knocked out! I got up to go retrieve the letter and it was from the academy; I thought to myself, '*Okay, before it's been what it's been but I'm going to think positive and I will keep being persistent.*' As soon as I opened it, I saw: "CONGRADULATIONS!" I didn't even finish reading the letter and I began praising the Lord doing my dance! I was dancing before this news because you are to praise Him before your blessing comes however this was a little more! *YESSSS!* I'm that much closer to my dreams becoming a reality.

The academy was tough as nails yet I pressed on with the mark of the high calling of Jesus Christ. He picked me up and carried me for sure; I almost felt like I couldn't go on. My father was pretty strict; I could get away with a few things and have him wrapped around my finger at times; here it wasn't happening and I appreciated it. This is what I needed to push me out of being complacent in my comfort zone. Out in the real world especially being a cop nobody cares who you are; people only see the uniform. The academy is 12 weeks; I was in basic training that consisted of classroom learning about the traffic laws and regulations, citations, report writing, learning about the New York City Criminal codes and psychology.

I didn't think there would ever be a psychology course in a police academy but there is a substantial amount of people with mental health issues in the streets; I asked my mom about some of the conditions since she is a psychologist and it helped me out a lot. I'm going to have to properly learn how to navigate and use persuasive action to retrieve a weapon from people who are harming themselves and others. We had driving courses and that was really fun for me! I could drive kind of fast and not get pulled over! I laughed to myself every time I was behind the wheel with this thought in mind. There's tactical training on how to properly physically arrest and put handcuffs on people; we had physical fitness courses and during one of the drills I met Qena. We were running side-by-side it seemed as if we were on one accord.

"Girl, you getting it in!" I said to her with short breaths.

"So are you!" Qena said panting, "I had to catch up; I felt I was dragging behind until I saw you and I had to pick up the pace!" Qena said with short breaths and we laughed.

Qena Jamson. I liked her name; I haven't heard it before. She has the most beautiful skin it reminded me of Africa when I saw her. She's 5'5", curvy, with medium-length dark-brown hair, high cheekbones, round brown eyes with a picture-perfect smile. Beautiful. Qena is from Houston, Texas. She told me she got her name from her mother when her parents went to visit Egypt; Qena is one of the cities there. Her mom said whenever she had a daughter that would be her name. We both have kindred spirits and got along well.

"Girl my bunions are on fire today!" Qena said as we sat down on the street curb at the end of another drill run; it was a long and dry day at the academy.

"Yeah, my side is hurting!" I said exhaustedly, "you would think I would be used to this by now but I'm not!" I said and we both laughed.

"Girl, what about when we add the belt with our equipment and especially the gun! That's an extra 15 pounds! So, you better get right!" Qena said as we both laughed.

"Yeah, that's true!" I said in agreement.

She turned to look at me and asked, "What made you join the force, Mist?"

"My grandfather and father were both detectives. I want to keep the legacy going. What's great is that I didn't need to be coaxed to pursue this career. I've always wanted to do it so that's why."

"What about you, Qena? Can I call you Q sometimes?" I asked her.

"Yeah, girl, everybody calls me that and it's cool. I have a cousin who is a police officer and he's been one since I was little. I've always been a peculiar and curious kid so I thought when I became older if I still have that same curiosity in me, I would go for it!" Qena said genuinely. I had great respect for her after hearing that. She has a go getter attitude; went for what she wanted and wasn't afraid to do so! We became sister friends and stuck by each other's side from that day forward.

It was time to go to the gun range! Now this is the part both Qena and I were most anxious about; carrying a weapon that is known for such horrendous acts and causes so many deaths is going to be entrusted to me. I have to be responsible and respect the weapon.

"Mist, how are you feeling?" Qena asked me nervously.

"I'm okay, it's a big step but we knew it was eventually coming and it's here! I'm trying to remain calm. Don't start tripping 'cause we both don't need to be tripping!" I said with butterflies in my stomach.

"You're right! I just need to breathe. I mean, we've come this far by faith, right?" Qena asked with a little confidence.

"Amen! Now you're speaking my language!" I said with excitement. We were given a Glock .45 Semi-Automatic Pistol. I've seen my father's gun. Although, he made sure to keep it locked and out of reach but to see it with *my eyes*; knowing that I'm going to be carrying my own was a little intimating. We all got suited up with the goggles and ear protection gear then began target practice. Everybody was doing a good job getting the just of everything. Qena was really into it! Now it was my turn to shoot. Once I picked up the gun, I felt an immediate connection; it's something that I can't explain fully but the sensation felt like lighting inside of my body. The gun wasn't too heavy or too light it fit perfectly in my hand. All of the anxiety melted away and I was able to stand tall, toe-to-toe with the piece. Aim and shoot at the target: "BOOM! BOOM! BOOM!" I shot three rounds and it felt good! I believe the reason why I felt so comfortable is because my intentions are to do well and to protect. The Lord knows this. He can trust me to do the right thing.

"OFFICER MISTY RIVERS!" I heard my name through the microphone when I walked up to receive my badge it was one of the greatest moments of my life. When I got my badge, we raised our right hands and took the oath. I was happy that the Lord saw me through it all! I was so excited and proud to wear my uniform. I wish you could've seen my parent's faces and mannerisms. The glimmer in my father's eye; I believe he even choked up a bit while my mother held her head so high, I thought she was Queen Elizabeth from Buckingham Palace. She is a queen to me. After the ceremony I introduced my family to Qena.

"Mom, Dad, and Ahmad, this is my bestie Qena," I said.

"Hello, Mr. and Ms. Rivers, it's a pleasure to finally meet you!" Qena said. My parents embraced her with a hug as my brother had to pick his mouth up from off the floor. "Congratulations to you sweetie! It's our pleasure to finally meet you too! We're so happy Missy had someone here with her and not have to go through the academy alone. We heard a lot of good things about you too!" my mom said.

Qena blushed and said, "Thank you Mrs. Rivers that means a lot."

"You bad girl! You make me wanna join the academy!" Ahmad said and everybody started laughing; Qena smiled and blushed.

"Are you going to stay in New York?" my dad asked Qena.

"For a little while then I want to transfer to Atlanta, Georgia," Qena said.

"That's great! We hope you get the chance to go!" my dad said happily. We all took pictures and had a wonderful dinner at my favorite restaurant. Everything was starting to fall in place.

Upon graduating from the academy, I was with field officers for four months; a different officer for each month. They took me out onto the street to teach me about the different addresses, how to answer the radio transmitter, more driving techniques and responding to calls. I was really writing citations for people now that I was out in the field and some people tried to persuade me to let them go but the law is the law. I tried to be nice to some but not all; I was not a push over. Being with the field officers was interesting; driving around and looking at the city from this prospective was life changing. There's so much to look out for that you can't ever be truly safe; everywhere you go danger awaits. Officer Dent was the strictest. He had to be; one false move and your life is gone! The Bible says in *James 4:14 Your life is but a vapor that appears for a little time and then vanishes away*. I thought Officer Dent was doing too much sometimes like if I left the car running too long, he was going to court-martial me! I just did what I was told, let him be and tried not ask him too many questions!

I became a patrol officer patrolling middle school and high school it was nice. Especially high school it's the most important time in your development; finding out what you want to do with your life after high school ends. Adulthood is up next and there's no mercy. I had the chance to talk to some of the girls on campus; they looked up to me and wanted to be in law enforcement one day. It empowered the young ladies to see a woman, short in stature and in her feminine energy to stand strong with my head held high. Wearing the uniform the right way earned you respect. Of course there were some teenagers' I had to put in check because they thought they could test me. I let them know crystal clear that if you step out of line *you* will be arrested and I wasn't afraid to do so.

One day I was patrolling an elementary school and I had my eye on this little girl. She reminded me of myself when I was little her name was Jill. She was about eight years old, had light brown skin, beautiful curly black hair and she looks of an Ethiopian decent. On this particular day I saw her sitting by herself on the bench outside of the cafeteria. She looked like she had something on her mind so I went to go check on her to see if she was okay.

I walked up next to her and asked, "Hi, Jill, are you okay?" She shook her head no. "Is it alright if I could sit next to you?" I asked. She nodded yes, I sat next to her and waited for her to speak; she sat there for a moment looking down at the ground.

She then said, "I'm so hungry, my mom and I are homeless and she can't get us anything to eat. I can't even get a school lunch because my mom doesn't have a job yet and we don't have an address for the school to send lunch tickets," she said all of this as she was crying and my heart was broken in two.

"Where does your mom go when you're at school?"

I asked her trying to hold back my tears. "She goes job hunting but she hasn't been able to find anything. We're staying at a shelter and we eat there for breakfast but after that I don't eat anything else until we go back at night. By then it's very little they have left because the shelter is overcrowded," she said.

"After school today bring your mother to me and I will talk to her; okay sweetheart. You don't have to worry about anything else!" I said and I brought her in for a hug.

"Do you know this song, *Yes, Jesus loves me*?" I asked. Her eyes lit up and she nodded yes. I said, "Okay let's sing it together. *Yesss Jesus loves me, Yesss Jesus Loves me, Yesss Jesus Loves me for the Bible tells me so*." I saw the light of hope in her innocent eyes. I said, "Jesus loves you, Jill, and your mom. I will do my best to help in any way that I can okay."

"Yes, Miss Misty!" After school Jill brought her mother right to me. I was standing afar off watching the kids get on the bus and watching the parents, guardians, cousins, friends, aunts, uncles, grandmas and grandpas come get their little ones.

"Miss Misty, this is my mommy!" Jill said.

"Hello, I'm Hannah, how are you?" Hannah asked.

"I'm doing good, nice to meet you; your daughter is so beautiful and well behaved!" I said.

"Thank you so much! I have to keep her in line I don't play with kids being disrespectful," Hannah said. She's about my height 5'3", Ethiopian ethnicity, black straight hair, medium brown skin; beautiful lady. She carried herself well and it didn't look like she nor her daughter were homeless but that's on the outside; you don't judge a book by its cover.

"That's great! It shows with her. I asked Jill to bring you over to me because I spoke with her this afternoon. Don't be upset with her she was letting me know about your situation. I'm not here to judge; I want to help you. I can get you in a work-study program that will offer you paid training and help you with affordable housing. Is that alright with you?" I asked.

"Oh, my goodness! Thank you so much! Wow this is wonderful"—she started to cry a little bit then she continued—"it's been a tough couple of months going through a divorce and nobody wants to help me. I just left everything to start over and leaped out on faith!" she said as she was wiping the tears from her eyes.

"I understand and it's going to be alright now—" as I shed a small tear—"it's the least I can do," I said as I handed her the paper with all the information she needed. "If you have any problems, you let me know and I'll take care of it! God Bless you both and I'll be checking in you guys and I know Jill will keep me posted," I said as I looked down at her sweet little face.

"Yes, we will and thank you again, Misty!" Hannah said.

"You're more than welcome!" We all embraced each other with a hug. Four months later Hannah moved to the Bronx in a studio apartment until she could save more money to move into a bigger place; she also got a permanent position for the state of New York as a social worker. Jill is taking dance lessons; she loves her new school and their new life. God is Good and I was so happy to be a blessing to someone.

My request came through to transfer to the East 54th Division Harlem Station. I was to report to Captain Joshua Castle. He's a Caucasian gentleman, with short blonde hair, humpty build, medium height 5'8"; he was fair and focused. He reminded me of Capt. Devane from the '80s police show I loved called "Hunter." In Looks and speech he was quite close. I was assigned a partner for my very first night shift at the precinct. My new partner is a Hispanic gentleman his name is Terry Garcia; medium height, 5'7", olive skin complexion with jet-black hair that was cut military style. Dark brown eyes, clean-shaven, humble smile and very nice looking. I could keep my focus because he was married and had a little boy. He had one other partner before me but his partner transferred to another division. Terry seemed to be a good guy, very professional and treated me with respect.

I believe he knew that as minorities him being a Hispanic and I being a Black female we were treated differently on the force at times but nevertheless we proved we belonged here. "To protect and to serve." I was a little nervous on my first ever night shift but I made sure I fasted and prayed for our safety.

When we left the captain's office and got into the police car, Terry calmly said, "I understand your nervousness; I was nervous too going out on my first night shift but all is well it should be a good night." It was a mid-cold night; the holidays were around the corner and people are out and about.

We drove around for about three hours in our assigned area. Then the transmitter went off. *L56 come in! There's a break in on 1002 Main Street; a lady is being held at gun point!"*

Terry picked up the walkie-talkie and responded, "This is L56 and we're on the way! Requesting for back up!" I don't know what got inside of me but I had no fear at that point. Terry turned on the siren and we were gone! Once we got there, back up hadn't arrived; we were first on the scene! The man was inside the house at the front window with a gun next to a woman's head. There was a small light inside so we could see their silhouettes.

Terry and I both drew our guns, we ran up to the front of the house and I shouted for the very first time, "NYPD DROP YOUR WEAPON AND PUT YOUR HANDS UP!"

The man hollers out the window, "I'M NOT GOING BACK TO JAIL!"

Terry shouts and tries to persuade the man, "COME OUT WITH YOUR HANDS UP! LET THE LADY GO AND COME OUT! WE WON'T SHOOT IF YOU DON'T SHOOT! WE NEED YOUR COOPERATION. NO BODY MOVES NOBODY GETS HURT! NOW DROP YOUR

WEAPON AND COME OUT WITH YOUR HANDS UP!"
I can feel these-fiery sensations all over my body, taking in
this whole scene; it's *for real* not a game! This is new
territory and it came alive. I was in this moment. No turning
back.

I thought to myself, '*I have to save this woman and this
man! God please let him cooperate!*' The man only listened
to us not saying a word; he slowly moved with the woman
and the gun still pointed at her head; he opened the front
door. Back up arrived and I had to block them out to focus
on this man.

The man shouted as I heard the woman sobbing, "IF I
CAN'T HAVE HER, NOBODY CAN…"

BOOM!

He shot the woman's head! I hollered a blood curling,
"NNNOOO!" Within a blink of an eye I fired my gun,
BOOM! BOOM! BOOM! Killing the man instantly. Terry
and I ran desperately up the few steps to the front door; he
kicked the gun from the man and I went straight to the
woman to see if she were still alive; checking for any sign
of a pulse; I found one on her neck! Blood was coming from
the side of her head and everything became so vivid in my
mind. I had never seen so much blood on a person nor a
dead body lying right next to me. A body I had to shoot to
kill in order to save another. Before I knew it, the
paramedics came to retrieve the lady. I literally had her
blood on my hands. It was the very first time I ever shot my
gun at someone and it most certainly won't be the last.

Chapter 5
The Knowledge

In the aftermath of the crime scene, all I could think about was the woman and the hell she must've endured with that man; a classic case of domestic violence. I felt I was in a haze and everything was moving in slow motion. Terry had helped me up and walked me back into the front seat of the car but before he pulled off, we sat in silence. I know it's important for me not to get emotionally attached to my job but it's more than just a job; it's life and death. If we didn't feel anything, then we don't have blood running through our veins. "Do you want me to take you home and pick you up tomorrow morning? You can pick up your car from the station then?" Terry asked quietly. I nodded yes. Nothing else was said the entire ride to my house. When I opened the door to my apartment before I walked in, I wept.

I still had her blood on my clothes. The smell, the gun residue, sweat that I was drenched in, along with the sounds of her screaming all came crashing down like a ton of bricks. I was grateful that we made it through, heartbroken of what transpired but also hopeful. I finally picked myself up off the floor from the doorway and closed it. I didn't even check my messages I only had enough strength to call my parents to let them know I was okay. I couldn't bring myself to tell them what happened but I know *they knew* something was wrong. They didn't press me; they were just happy I was all right. I may call my brother tomorrow if I'm feeling up to it but it's a big "*IF.*" I needed to get out of these clothes and go to bed. I had a lot to think about and with the very last ounce of strength for the night I got on my knees and spoke to my Heavenly Father intensely. I don't care whatever happens in the day the Lord will always have His praises in my mouth and have my bending knee no matter how I feel; from the rising of the sun, to the going down of the same. It was displayed tonight that tomorrow, minutes and seconds are not promised to you. With one shot that woman's life changed forever; one decision that man made, one call that Terry and I answered changed the dynamics of our lives either for good or for the worse.

The Lord allowed me to sleep peacefully through the night. For God's mercies renews every morning I was able to get up the next day but my soul was really heavy. I thought to myself, '*as much faith as I have, how can I be in such a dark place?*' It doesn't matter if you're saved or not you will go through the darkness but as believers, we will be able to endure and know that God's grace is sufficient. My mom has said this to me numerous times and now I get it. I understand now what Officer Thomas was going through mentally after the 9/11 attacks. I stayed in bed a little longer, I was glad the captain told Terry and I that we could come in later and not give me the day off. If I did, I would wallow and stay in bed from being depressed. I really have a strong dislike for the word depressed along with the feelings that come with it however; you can't sweep your emotions under the rug. I allow myself to feel those emotions and go through what I need too; I don't stay in it. You can drown and most of the time people die because they can't get out of it. I can say I do feel awful and this too shall pass; I'm going to go talk to my pastor!

Terry came to pick me up and he looked tired too but we still pressed on. While sitting in the passenger seat I turned to look at him and said lovingly, "I'm happy you made it home last night to your family. Thank you for having my back."

"You're welcome and that's what partners do," he said calmly. When we got to the station it seemed to not miss a beat with the same pace and space.

Capt. Joshua wanted to speak with us. "Terry and Misty, you both handled yourself accordingly. I want you both to remain on the night shift because you responded quickly; you guys went in and worked together as a team.

I know the outcome wasn't what either of you expected but that's the job! It's unpredictable. So, until further notice I'll be watching you two and especially you, Misty. I know that was your first shoot out. Are you okay?"

"Yeah!" I belted out. Deep down I wasn't but I knew where I could get the help.

"Okay, go get yourselves together for your shift tonight," Capt. Joshua said.

I was driving and thinking. The car is where I have most of my conversations with the Lord among other places; thinking about what happened that night. I needed the knowledge from that experience to be able to understand my mission; my purpose for being in this field; but most importantly I need the knowledge of God. I asked Him for help with my mental capacity to be able to withstand dire consequences on the job. In Psalms 46:1 it tells us that *God is our refuge and strength, a very present help in trouble.* I didn't think I would ever feel this way but I'm at a crossroads. I can't let fear take control and let it get in the way of what the Lord has for me. I didn't feel it in the moment but once the adrenaline wore off, it crept in. Fear can be sneaky and can sneak up on you just when you thought you had conquered it. That's why I *need* the Lord; He doesn't give you the spirit of fear; I *need* His Holy Spirit to guide and teach me because I don't know what I'm doing.

This assignment is bigger than me. I feel like David facing Goliath but David won and I'll win too; I just have to go through the wilderness first. I drove to my church to speak with my pastor. I've been a member ever since the day Elaine and I walked in; it's been a couple of years now. Pastor Jeremiah Hughes Sr. and his wife First Lady Ava Hughes are younger; still old school with a new school twist. They welcomed me with open arms. I'm a part of the prayer ministry and with the missions as they go to the shelters to donate food.

Pastor is tall 6'4", James Bond 007 handsome, Vanilla complexion, with a sly dynamite smile with an air of compassion, Godliness, wisdom and love. He's authentic, cares about his congregation and loves his wife and family.

Ava is half his size about 5'2", she is of Hispanic decent with olive skin like Terry, with dark brown hair and delicate facial features. She's beautiful, poised, intelligent and kind. I was very happy that the pastor had a few moments to be able to speak with me today. We sat in the front pew of the sanctuary. When the pastor started speaking, I immediately felt peace in my spirit; his voice was light as air. "I whole-heartedly know how you feel, Sister Misty. I also suffered from post-traumatic stress syndrome after I came home from the war. I was an army solider in desert storm and when I came home, I was a wreck. I didn't know the Lord then. My mother and father took me to church; my mother was a part of the hospitality services and my father was involved in the men's ministry. I've had awareness but I wasn't serious about my faith. After going through that experience in the war I know the Lord lead me to giving my life to Him! Also having praying parents because I was losing my mind. I didn't know where to go or who to turn too. They didn't have mental health experts to help us navigate how to deal with life once the war was over. A lot of my friends turned to drugs and even committed suicide God Bless their souls. Later on my family and I found people and organizations to be able to help me get back on track. It took a massive amount of time and patience. You have to be patient with yourself. Time heals wounds, a willingness to move forward and deal with the issues at hand. That's why the Lord tells us the battle is not ours; it's His! It's tough because the human nature in us wants to fix things. The fact that you have the Lord in your life during this trial you're going through is a huge stepping-stone, Sister Misty! Know that *you* know the Lord is with you every step of the way. God said in *Deuteronomy 31:8 He will never leave nor forsake you.*

Don't be afraid to ask for help if you need it. God's got your back!"

I could feel the Holy Spirit rise inside of me during this whole conversation. I was crying and listening; taking in every word. I spoke softly while sniffing, "Pastor Jeremiah; thank you! I'm very grateful that you shared a personal story about yourself so I could see you as a person. It means more than you could ever know…thank you! Thank you so much!"

"Sister Misty, we're here for you in any way we can. If you need anything, please let us know."

"Thank you, Pastor Jeremiah. I will!" I said with gratitude.

"Sister Misty, let's say a prayer before you leave," Pastor Jeremiah said.

We stood up, bowed our heads, closed our eyes and he touched my shoulder while I lifted my hands in praise as he began. *"Father, Father God we ask for your forgiveness today! Please forgive us of our sins. Your daughter, Misty, Father God is going through a tough time but you said Lord, you are there with us. Lord, you said in Matthew 18:20 For where two or three are gathered together in my name, there I am in the midst of them. We thank you, Jesus, for being the ultimate sacrifice and shedding your blood so that we would have access to our father God. You Jesus took the yoke and the heavy burdens so that we could live Lord God! Live to be able to fight another day in you Lord; we will win and be victorious! Satan, I rebuke you in the name of Jesus Christ! Get thee behind and out of Sister Misty's mind; you have no place there! Hallelujah, Hallelujah! We thank you Lord that it's already done! Lord only you know what's next for Sister Misty. Please keep and protect her along with her partner Terry and the whole police precinct Father God. We ask this in Jesus Mighty Name! Thank God. Amen!"*

I left the church with my soul feeling lighter as if the burden had been lifted off my back; I was ready to face whatever it is that's awaiting me. Terry found out the hospital where the injured woman was being held at and I decided to visit. I went through security, showed my badge and said, "Hello, I'm Officer Misty Rivers. There was a lady that came in from last night's incident on Main Street."

"Oh yes!" the security officer said as he looked at the chart and found her room number. "That's room number 257; her name is Natalie Falcon; she's still in the ICU unit," the security officer said as he handed me a bright green sticker pass to put on my coat.

"Thank you, officer have a good day," I told him.

"Same to you, Officer Misty." The nurses were nice to assist me to the room. I stood in the doorway looking at her from afar. There she was in critical condition. Wires, IV drips and a breathing tube were in her mouth with bandages around her head. It was a very sad sight but I was still hopeful looking at her. I thought to myself, '*The Lord isn't done with her!*' I took a deep breath and said a silent prayer. When the nurse came in to check her IV drip, she let me know her condition without having to ask.

"She's pulling through! The bullet didn't penetrate her skull it went under the skin across the front of her head and out the other side. She's not brain dead; thank God. She may not remember all of what happened to her but she'll make it!"

"Thank you, nurse…?"

"I'm sorry; my name is Sarah."

"Thank you, Sarah. I'm Misty, nice to meet you and thank you for the information."

"Your more than welcome, Misty, nice to meet you too!" I took one last look at her; feeling relieved knowing she's going to be all right and left.

"I need all hands-on deck! We have a riot on our hands people and it's time to get into position!" Capt. Joshua said in a hasty and alarming tone. It was mid-day; summertime and it was slightly warm outside with a nice breeze. The captain was hyped and ready; I was too! Terry and I hurried up to put our gear on to get to Harlem; the riot wasn't far from my house on Malcolm X Blvd. A young 12-year-old black boy was shot and killed by the *police*, which made it worse. For the life of me I don't know why it still keeps on happening but it does.

The boy took a detour from his usual way home and was stopped by the police officer. The kid ran and the police chased him for no reason. Once they cut him off, he stopped and had his hands up; sure enough a trigger-happy cop shot him to death! The officer claims it was a mistaken identity because there was a robbery going on in the same part of town. This is what made my job really hard; these are my people that are being killed by the hands of law enforcement. How could I stand here with a badge as well and act like these officers aren't in the wrong! I simply can't do it! What I will do is go to the riot with the intentions of having my communities back and to bring order because I agree with them but the protest should be peaceful. Also letting them know that most of us are here to protect and to serve even though some of us aren't! "Misty, let's go!" Terry said urgently. Terry was driving like a mad man to the riot, he felt the same way too but we both knew that we have to keep our heads on straight. Once he pulled up it was a mess!

People were everywhere with signs protesting, looting and fighting! I had on my bulletproof vest with a face shield on just in case a smoke bomb had to be thrown to break up the crowd. When I stepped out the car, Terry and I split up! I went to the stores to stop the looting; I didn't have my gun out only my stick shouting as loud as I could. "EVERYBODY GET OUT OF HERE! YOU WILL BE ARRESTED! OUT NOW!" Some were leaving while some had to give me a hard time.

"SHUT UP PIG! SHUT THE HELL UP! WE AIN'T LEAVING PIG!" Men and women were saying this to me from every angle. I remained in my element and stood up to them; I shouted again loudly!

"PLEASE! I DON'T WANT TO SHOOT ANYONE! EVERYBODY OUT! THAT'S MY LAST WARNING!" More left but there were a few that didn't. I pulled out my gun and shot twice in the air!

BOOM! BOOM!

"EVERYBODY OUT NOW!" I shouted at the top of my lungs! Everybody left! I cleared one store. There were more people scattered in other places as I looked through the windows. When I walked out, Terry ran right up to me!

"MIST, ARE YOU ALRIGHT?" he yelled.

"YES!" I shouted. It was so loud and reckless; I've never been in a riot! I've seen it on television; never up close but here I am actually on the other end of the rope as an officer trying to keep the peace!

"COME ON, MIST! WE GOTTA GO TO THE OTHER STORES!" Terry shouted. I started running behind him. I tripped over someone and fell on my right arm where the gun dropped out of my hand! Terry turned around quickly; picked it up, helped me get on my feet and gave me back my gun. I turned around to see if the person was okay; it was an older man and he was beaten up badly. "TERRY, I HAVE TO HELP HIM! I WILL MEET YOU BY THE CAR IN A LITTLE WHILE!" I shouted.

"OKAY!" he said as he ran off to fight more people out of the stores and to keep them in line. I helped the gentleman up and I put his arm around my neck as he limped and I walked back to the police car. People were running everywhere; some police are beating people with sticks, while some are trying to help the women with children! Shots are being fired and smoke bombs are going off; it was a mini war zone! Screams, sirens and the angry rampage of people were mind blowing! When we finally reached the car, I opened the back door to lay him down in the backseat. I opened the front door, climbed in the seat and grabbed the transmitter walkie-talkie and shouted! "THIS IS L56! WE

NEED AN AMBULANCE RIGHT AWAY ON MALCOLM X BLVD! A MAN IS SEVERLY INJURED!"

"*L56! Ambulance is on its way!*"

the dispatcher responded. While I waited, I looked up at the street sign with Malcolm X's name on it. It brought me back to when I first came on this block and how I was so happy to be a part of history; not knowing in a few years I would be on the front lines of a riot! I know Malcolm would be extremely disappointed by the fact of people looting and fighting amongst each other over the same racial prejudices that he was fighting against almost sixty years ago! On the other hand he was a revolutionary and he believed *we,* as black people *should* fight back against injustice as most people are doing here today; the right way!

We stayed in the car for a few minutes then the ambulance showed up. As I led them to where the man was, I heard, "Excuse me, Miss, your arm doesn't look good," the guy paramedic said to me.

"I'm fine! I need to get back out there!" I said as I shrugged him off.

"Miss, please your arm looks broken!" the guy paramedic said in a concern tone.

I was such in an adrenaline rush that I didn't even realize I was hurt let alone my arm could be broken! As soon as the medic touched my right arm I yelled, "AHHHHHH! OH MY GOD! OH MY GOD!"

"Calm down, Miss!" the guy paramedic said. As the other medic was tending to the man this one led me to the back of the truck as well. The riot seemed to have died down a little. I hadn't seen Terry in a minute; I hope he was okay!

About 45 minutes later my arm was bandaged up and Terry finally came jogging to the A-Car.

"Are you alright, Mist? Is your arm going to be okay?" he asked calmly.

"Yeah! I have to go get some x-rays done but I'm hanging in there! Are you alright, Terry?" I asked and gave him a smile.

"Yeah! I'm good. I'm hanging in there too!" he said and smiled back. We found out that it was 25 arrested, 10 people shot and 15 people injured. I was grateful that we made it! No deaths were reported; I was relieved there wasn't but heartbroken that we continue to go through these same issues; nevertheless, God is still on the throne.

"I'm so proud of you, Jo!" Ahmad said.

"Thank you, Ahmad!" My phone has been ringing non-stop since the riot. It was all over the news; everywhere!

"I'm going to start calling you 'Superwoman' for helping that man while having the courage to stand up to the people! That's amazing, sis! I'm glad you weren't badly hurt though. What did the doctors say about your arm?" he asked.

"Me too, you're so funny! I have a stress fracture; it's a small hairline crack; it's hard to spot in an x-ray but it's still swollen and tender. I'll be fine." It felt good hearing his voice and the support that everybody has been giving; not just to me but to the whole team. We all tried our best to handle the situation and maintain peace.

"I'm glad it's not broken! I know Mom and Dad were worried; how are you doing?" he asked.

"I spoke to them right before you called and they're better. I'm okay still recovering from the incident. They know what my job requires but in the end I'm still their daughter as they always tell me."

"No doubt, Jo! I hope you're going to take it easy and chill for a little while!" he said.

"Captain gave me two weeks off and more time if I need it so the arm could heal."

"That's cool, sorry I couldn't make it up to see you but I'll be there soon!" he said.

"It's okay, bro, I know you'll come if the Lord is willing," I said.

"Yes, indeed, sis! Yes indeed!" he said in agreement. "Okay, sis, I'm headed back to class; I'm almost done! I'll call you tomorrow," he said excitedly.

"Yesss! I'm so proud of you too! Can't wait till you get your master's degree; you have worked extremely hard for it! You deserve it, bro!"

"Thank you, Jo! I appreciate you. I love you," Ahmad said.

"Love you too!" Talking to my brother always makes me feel warm inside; can't believe I used to change his diapers! All jokes aside we were raised to respect one another and that's what we do.

One hour later. *Ring, Ring…* "Hello!" I said as I answered the phone.

"GIRLL! What's going on up there?" Elaine asked, in her bossy voice.

"I know right! It's been crazy?" I said.

"How are you feeling?" Elaine asked.

"Much better! I spoke to my brother a little while ago before you called."

"That's good! How's he doing? I know *he's fine* now; good Lord!" Elaine said flirtatiously.

"And you know this!" I said and we both laughed.

"He's doing good!"

"How are your parents? I know they were tripping?" Elaine asked.

"Yeah, but they calmed down once they heard my voice."

"I know they did! Well, girl, I'm coming up! I haven't seen you in a while and it's time! I hate that it had to be under these circumstances but I'll be there on Wednesday morning and staying until Sunday!" Elaine said with excitement. I walked over to my mail table and checked my little calendar: today is Monday June 10!

"That's awesome, I'm glad you're coming!" My voice went up a notch as if I was 15 again by the thought of her being here. "YES! YES, GIRL! COME ON!" I couldn't contain myself.

"Okay! I'll see you soon! I love you, Miss!" Elaine said ecstatically.

"Love you too, Elaine!"

30 minutes later.

Ring. Ring…

"Hello!" I said as I answered the phone.

"Hey lady what's up? How are you?" Qena asked excitedly; her voice sounded as smooth as silk. "You know I saw the riot! Did you have your cape on trying to be a Superwoman?"

"GIRLL! I wasn't trying to. *I was!*" We both laughed but Qena got serious.

"For real lady I'm so happy to hear your voice and I'm glad you're alright," Qena said.

"I'm hanging Q; I really am."

"How's the family?" Qena asked.

"Everyone is well! How's your family and the little one doing?"

"Harley is ten months old now!" Qena said like a proud new mom.

"I can't believe it's been ten months already; she's going to be in middle school within a blink of an eye!" I said happily.

"I know. It's scary!" Qena said.

"How's your husband Ian?" I asked.

"He's great! Being Ian as usual but he's fine. I was calling to let you know that I'm coming to see you!" Qena said ecstatically.

This was a double blessing! I was so overjoyed to know that my two best friends were coming to visit and they could finally meet each other for the first time.

"Remember my friend Elaine I told you about?" I asked Qena.

"Yes, I remember," she said.

"She's coming on Wednesday! I just got off the phone with her not to long ago!"

God is so good He knew I needed my sisters to come and see me! "That's great, lady! I can't wait to meet her and give you all a big hug!" Qena said.

"This is something that we all need," I said.

"Yes, and I know it was due to the unfortunate event that I made this move but it won't be like this anymore; for something negative to happen for me to come see you," Qena said sincerely.

"I know you have a family and you work the force too, Q! I understand and yes when we all get together, we're going to make it our business to at least plan three times out of the year to visit one another!" I said.

"I agree! I'll be there Thursday afternoon on June 13th and stay until Sunday!" she said.

"Perfect! Elaine will be here the day before on Wednesday the 12th and you are both leaving on the same day! WOW, you guys are *NSYNC and haven't even met yet! That's how God works!" I said laughing with assurance.

"You better believe it! I love you and I'll see you soon!" she said.

"YESS! I love you too, Q."

I haven't laughed so much and so hard in a little while. When we all got together, I felt the sisterhood that I never knew I needed but God did. Qena and Elaine fit together like a puzzle. What they had in common was their love for me. It's amazing how I met both of them at very important stages of my life; Elaine my childhood and Qena my adulthood. They didn't feel intimidated by one another and that was a blessing. We went to this spa called; *RELAX* located in upper Manhattan in this plush skyscraper not far from the Empire State Building. *RELAX* was an upscale spa. When we opened the glass doors, we were welcomed with beautiful artwork in the foyer; it smelled like the perfect combination of lavender and mint. The receptionist was behind a beautiful white marble desk and was well dressed with a cream-colored blazer with the word *RELAX* on the right side. Next to the desk was a glass cabinet with candles, soaps and oils for purchase. We walked up to the desk.

"Good afternoon, welcome to *RELAX*. I'm Vera, do you have an appointment?" Vera asked.

"Yes, Rivers for three," I said.

I turned to face my sisters with my back against the desk and said, "I've wanted to come here for a while; I'm so happy I get to share this experience with my sistas!" As I wrapped my left arm around Elaine, Qena followed suit since I only had one arm and she closed the gap by putting her arm on my right side making it a group hug!

"I still can't believe we're all here; we get to have a mini vacation together. I really needed this; this feels so wonderful!" I said to Qena and Elaine as I was sitting in the middle of them; we were all in the Jacuzzi after our massages. I had to put my arm on the outside of the ledge because of the bandages but that didn't stop me from enjoying the moment.

"Me too and you've got to start taking it easy and finding the time for yourself, Miss," Elaine said to me.

"She's right! You have to force yourself to treat yourself," Qena said.

I nodded in agreement listening to what my sisters where saying. Elaine turned and looked at me directly in the eyes and said with love. "Even though we just met each other; Qena and I. We both know how hard you are on yourself; you want to be the best you can be and get the job done; that's in you. You're a police officer in one of the biggest and most dangerous cites in the world; you know this but you are my sister and I want to make sure you're all right to carry such a load. That's why I'm here to let you know that you're not alone!" Elaine said to me with fire in her eyes; it made me cry happy tears.

Qena put her arm around me; I turned my face to her and she said, "Amen! I'm here for you too, Miss, because you and I both know how this job is but it's more than that. We were called for this line of work; it's our calling and just like Elaine said we carry a load but we have to know when to let go and let God! The Lord says we are to comfort one another and share each other's burdens and that's what we're here for."

It was the most therapeutic moment next to my pastor's prayer. We all hugged and cried happily. In *Romans 12:2 It tells us to not be conformed to this world; but be ye transformed by the renewing of your mind, that ye may prove what is that good, and acceptable, and perfect, will of God.* That's what this visit did for me; it renewed my mind and I'm quite sure my sisters felt the same. The next day we went to church and I introduced my sisters to my pastor and 1st lady; even though Elaine already met them when she helped me find the church, she was happy to see them again. As I came home from seeing the girls off from the airport, I sat on my couch and reflected on our time together. I was so full of love and refreshed. I felt myself come from out of the dark cloud that I was under for a while; having my sisters here was truly an honor and very much appreciated. God always knows what you need before you do. I'm grateful to Him and for them.

Ring…Ring!

I reached for the phone in a slothful manner; I was so relaxed.

"Hello! Hi, Mommy," I said warmly.

"Missy baby, how are you?" my mom asked ever so sweetly.

"I'm doing better, Mom. How are you?"

She was quiet.

"Hello!" I said curiously.

"Yes, baby, I'm here. I wanted to let you know…the doctors found a lump in my breast."

Chapter 6
Detective Misty Rivers

Before my mom had the chance to utter the words, "Baby don't come." I was on the next plane to North Carolina; I wanted to be at her next appointment. My dad is there but I know he's not taking this well; I called Ahmad once I landed and he'll be here in a few days.

Q

"Breast cancer, Mom? Did you get a second opinion?" I asked my mother in a hasty tone as I sat next to her on the couch.

"Three of them! Missy, I don't want you all worrying about me!" my mother said.

"Oh Lord, Mom, that's not it! We're here for support and no I'm not worried; I'm concerned." Dad was quiet; he was quiet when we drove from the airport. When he picked me up, he was very relieved and happy to see me; I could see the stress in his face. He's hiding it from me and it's okay. My mom is his world just like all of us. A man of his character won't open up much; he would peel back his layers in time when he's ready.

Coming back to work after my mother's appointment was heart wrenching. The doctors said her cancer is treatable; she will have to undergo chemotherapy four days a week for at least a year. If it gets worse, she may lose her left breast. I had to drag myself to work the next couple of weeks. It was a usual day but I thank the Lord Terry and I made it back in one piece. I was more than ready to get home and relax because I had a few extra days off from working non-stop. On this particular day as I was leaving the station the captain nearly ran out of breath trying to find me. He handed me an envelope. He didn't say anything but I could see his face was happy; his disposition felt positive and I received it. On my way up the stairs to my apartment thoughts were shuffling in my head. I didn't think I would ever question or reconsider what I wanted to be in my life but these past couple of months have put my faith to the test in ways I couldn't even imagine.

This time made me appreciate the journey and I have gained a lot of perspective from the shooting, speaking to my pastor, going through the riot, having my girlfriends meet for the first time with all of us together. Praying without ceasing, having quiet nights alone and my mom's diagnosis to top it off; it all became clear. I've made my decision. When I walked into my apartment, I laid today's mail on my famous coffee table while holding on to the envelope the captain gave me. I went to sit down on the couch and I finally opened it; I read the very first line: *I recommend Officer Misty Rivers for detective school.*

"Ahmad, what do you think?" I asked my little brother. He came to New York for a surprise visit from California and it melted my heart. I needed him right now.

"Yeah, Jo, that's what's up! It's about time for you to step up and make detective now. I can't imagine the things you've gone through to get to this point!" he said while he was squeezing out mustard from a condiment packet in his sandwich. We were having lunch in Central Park. It was a cool day also warm enough for us to sit and have some sandwiches on a bench. There wasn't a lot of people here only enough to go around.

"Oh, bro, if only you knew! I mean; you do but I could only express so much over the phone. To actually witness it in person is another thing! You knew I had depression for a little while." I took a moment to think about that. I really try not to use that word; it's like spoiled milk…yuck! But it is what is.

"I understand. Dealing with the pressures of being an engineer is stressful as well! Especially when you feel like no one wants to work or help you. Some people don't want *you* to get further than them and end up taking their job!" Ahmad said with an agitated tone.

"I remember the story you told me about that situation; did you ever get the chance to talk to the board of directors?" I asked intently.

"No! Not yet. I have a hearing in a week and I can't wait! I have everything I need to get my point across. I'm always asking myself this question, '*Why does it have to be this way?*' Then I think about what Dad said to us, '*We have to work twice as hard and, in this case, quadruple the work!'* I'm able and willing to do whatever it takes because no one is going to stop me from being an engineer at NASA," my brother said with assurance and confidence.

"I know that's right, bro! I'm so proud of you! I can't say it enough!" I said beaming with pride.

"Thank you! I'm proud of you too, Jo! You inspire me; your strength is without measure. I hope to find a lady one day that displays the same strong faith," my brother said to me genuinely; I almost wanted to cry. I reached out my left arm and brought him in for an embrace. When we pulled away, we looked at each other; I could *see* my brother is becoming a real man. God fearing, courageous, smart, friendly, GQ handsome, tall and loves chasing women! I'm glad that whatever he does it doesn't get in the way of his studies; he's living his life to the fullest. His phone started blowing up!

"So, who's the lucky girl?" I asked being nosy.

"You mean; the lucky *GIRLS?*" he said and we busted out laughing. I'm happy that my bro and I could talk about anything. He has his privacy of course and I have the utmost respect for it. We have our fallouts and disagreements as siblings do but nothing in this world can keep us apart.

"I know you have patiently waited for this day to come. I'm so excited for you," my mom said to me while we're at her Chemo appointment. She was relaxed and peaceful; I could tell she has been doing a lot of praying. That's who she is. As I sat looking at her while the IV is in her arm with the nurses coming in checking back and forth, I remembered the scripture from *Philippians 4:11 Saying to be content where you are*. It's amazing that during my deepest and darkest thoughts the Lord *never* fails to show me the light in His word. How could I be content on seeing my mother whom is everything to me laying here with a health battle? Chemo pumping into her veins to get rid of the cancer cells from deteriorating her body.

Then I think about what Jesus went through. His suffering and He's the light of the world however God made Him a prime example. The Bible tells us in *Isaiah 53:5 He was wounded for our transgressions and by His stripes we are healed.* That's in the word! We must suffer; it's a suffering way there's no doubt about it but there's also healing.

"Missy baby, I'm so happy you're here with me today," my mom said as she smiled with her eyes.

"Mom, you know I'll be here whenever I can. I'm happy that Dad and Ahmad are able to come. We seem to have put together a good system and that's great! We're all participating in helping you get well," I said while holding her hand.

"Yes, your father is better. We've had our talks, prayer sessions and sometimes we sit and hold one another. I truly believe the closeness that we share has been great medicine. There are times when I'm too weak to get up and your father steps in the best way he knows how." Then my mother sat up straighter, looked me dead in my eyes and said, "I need for you to understand that whatever is going on with me I don't want it to affect you from focusing on your schooling. Can you hand me my purse, baby?"

I reached on the opposite side of me and handed it to her. She pulled out a black velvet square box and handed it to me. I opened it and it was a 24k gold magnifying glass with Swarovski crystals on the handle. It was the most beautiful thing I've ever seen. I looked up at her; my eyes filled with tears and she continued, "You get your head right and go get your blessing! Do you understand me?" my mother said with passion.

I nodded and said, "Yes, ma'am." The tears flowed down as she wiped my cheek. My mother gave her blessing. Remember what I said in the beginning about becoming a detective was the greatest pain of my life; how the pain makes it great. My mother at the time was in unfathomable excruciating physical pain and I was in mental painful anguish watching her go through this but she assured me to go and complete the assignment that the Lord has for me. In my state of mind I didn't see a way but God does; He gave me the confirmation I needed through my mother's pain to keep pressing on as Jesus did for us!

Learning about the forensic science of DNA in detective school was fascinating; it was great because my focus is to be a Homicide detective. Anything you touch your print is on it. You could leave a strand of hair at a crime scene and it could possibly solve the case! That's mind-boggling! There's a course on evidence recovery; which is my strong point because I love searching for clues and you never have too many. The devil is in the details and I'm very detail oriented. At a crime scene you need to retrieve every piece of clothing, thread, leaf or paper surrounding the area. They taught photography and showed me how to take pictures of the crime scene. This course was intense because of what happened earlier in my career as a patrol cop. I had to make a life-or-death decision and having to take a photo of a deceased person knowing that their loved one is gone is very disturbing; it made this particular class personal. There was also crime scene drawing. I've seen the sketch of the fugitive my father was trying to find who killed his police friends; they didn't have a photo of the guy and was going off of an eyewitness observation. I would also see this on the news and on crime shows. I rarely see it anymore but now I get to try it! I never knew it was a part of the detective process; this course brought out the artist in me.

My teacher was Mrs. Geraldine Santana she was about seventy years old, stood 4'8" with white platinum hair, big round, black glasses, flawless olive skin, and was always beautifully dressed. She's traveled all over the world and took her art seriously; she was like a Picasso artist. She's been teaching the class for twenty years and has been on some of the most well-known cases in history. It was an honor to be a part of her class. I learned how to do technical writing and here's an in-depth example of what it consisted of: When you write your case up, it goes over to the prosecutor. They read that information and determine based on the information that *you* provide in the technical report, if the prosecutor would even attempt to prosecute the case. It's taking information that the officer gives you, going back and doing a follow up on *wha*t the officer gave you, then putting it into a report to send to a prosecutor.

Basically, double-checking whatever information I get is correct before the report goes to the prosecutor. With all of this knowledge, training and experience I was finally ready to take the test. I fasted and prayed for three days and made sure I got enough sleep.

Three weeks later I checked the mail and there was the letter: Detective School of New York City. I tried not to think about how I did but I just knew I aced the exam. I opened it right there in the hallway of my apartment building and it read: *We regret to inform you; your test scores did not meet the criteria of the detective post.* I had to read it again to make sure I knew what I was reading was true. I failed the exam!

"Missy baby, you can try again!" my mom said to me as I was pacing the living room floor in disbelief. I actually failed the test; it was a huge blow to the gut!

"Baby don't get yourself worked up it happens! I didn't pass the first time either!" my dad said as he was sitting on the couch next to my mom. I stopped dead in my tracks.

"You didn't tell me that, Dad!" I said to him in shock as I sat down on the recliner across from them. "Really, Dad!"

"Really, baby! It's tricky; you have to take it a second time in order for you to pass it because you get a feel of the flow and familiarity of the test. I didn't want to tell you until after you had taken it. I know how you are; you're like me.

You wanna do it the first time around. You can on something's but on other things you have to take it again! It's alright. I know it's hurtful and that you've worked so hard; be strong and of good courage baby. We know you can do it and *you* know it too! Take your time 'cause I know you rushed through it like a tornado! It's yours, baby girl!" my dad said in an uplifting voice. I didn't say a word; I just took everything my parents was saying to me at face value because they're right. It's mine and I'm going to win!

Two weeks later I received the same envelope in the mail. I hurried up with even more anticipation from the last letter and it read: *"Congratulations you have successfully exceeded the exam. You'll receive an additional certificate for a perfect score result."*

"DETECITVE MISTY RIVERS!" I heard my name from the microphone during the award ceremony. As I was walking up, I felt I was now walking into my God ordained purpose. When I shook the captain's hand and I looked over to see my family in the crowd, I could see the glory of the Lord all over them. My mother Mrs. Inez Rivers; her glow starting to come back and whose pain brought me thus far. My father Detective Andrew Rivers, he's the reason why I'm here; my brother Ahmad Rivers for his unwavering faith, and my two sister friends Elaine and Qena; one on my

117

left side and the other on my right. I said to myself, '*Life is good!*'

Chapter 7
A Father's Love

Ring…Ring!

"Detective Rivers," I said as I answered the phone at my desk. There was a pause; I reached over and grabbed my mug to take a swig of my hot lemon tea.

"Hello, gorgeous," the voice said. I almost choked on my tea! From my bewildering amazement I didn't think I would ever get a call from this someone. Someone who I haven't thought about in years, someone that only my parents would give information about my whereabouts, someone who made my soul feel good.

It was Cory Kinsmen.

"Hi! Cory!" I said nervously. Honestly, I haven't talked to a man on this level since Ocean. I flirted and had my eye on a few gentlemen but it seemed that anyone who I was remotely attracted to either had a girlfriend or a wife.

So, I just let it go, dived into my work and making my dreams come into fruition. I want to fall in love; I'm a young woman. I have morals and I've been doing my best to live soberly and in celibacy but it's tough. I asked him curiously as I squinted my eyes, "How do you get this number?"

Cory said, "When I went to visit my grandma a week ago, I went to see your folks as well and say hello. I asked if I could have your number and your mom gave it to me."

"Of course she did!" I said sarcastically.

"How have you been? I hope I'm not disturbing you?" he asked in his baritone sexy voice.

"No! No! Not disturbing me at all," I said nonchalantly; knowing good and well I could feel the heat sensations running over my body.

"I'm well! How are you?" I asked him.

"I'm better now that I'm talking to you," he said coyly. I could've burst inside but I had to remain calm. I couldn't let on that I was over the moon!

"Oh! Is that right?" I asked with cockiness.

"Yes, that's right!" Cory said with the most sexist infectious laugh I've have ever heard. He sounded the same but with a dash of age. It's expected since we are full-fledged adults now. I almost got tongue-tied! I managed to muster out a flirty laugh and I had to catch myself because I was at work. "Congratulations on making detective; I know that's been your dream," Cory said.

"Thank you! Yeah, it's been a tough road but with God's help He made it happen," I said.

"I hear you!" Cory said.

"What career path did you end up choosing?" I asked.

"I'm in commercial real estate. Are you single?" Cory asked.

"Yes; are you single?" I asked.

"Divorced; for five years now. We didn't have any children together we just grew apart. There's no bad blood between us. Some people aren't meant to be together; it happens!" he said modestly.

"I'm sorry about your divorce. I'm glad you're cordial toward each other; that's a good thing. Ummm… Let me have your number so I can call you after work," I said.

"Alright it's (206) 213-1955," he said as I jotted down his number on a note pad.

"Great! I'll call you when I get home around…7, okay? Talk to you soon!" I said in my most confident womanly voice.

"I'll be waiting," he said and hung up the phone. I still had the phone in my hand until I slowly put it down on the desk.

I thought to myself, '*Did that just happen? Yes, it did!*'

I moved into a new one-bedroom apartment in Brooklyn on 106th and Park Pl! It's an older complex like my first apartment because New York's buildings are old but it's updated with a fresh new paint job, new windows, new hardwood floors plus it's much bigger! There are stairs of course but there is an elevator when it wants to work; since I lived on the 5th floor it's not too bad. I felt grateful with the fact that I was moving up and having been able to accomplish what the Lord set out for me to do. It was a great feeling! I had the same set up as my studio apartment but there was an actual bedroom where I could close a door now; I had a view of the city lights instead of the next apartment building across from me.

When my parents, brother and girlfriends came to visit my last place, we would all pack in like sardines; it was good because we love each other and we're women. However, when my father and brother would come, I arranged for them to have their privacy; otherwise it was a big slumber party. I even bought new furniture and a new small four-piece dining set. I was excited to have a table now so I could have traditional dinners or host a dinner party! I kept my dinner trays in case I wanted to sit in front of the TV. Everything was coming together as *the Lord says in Romans 8:28 All things work together for good to them that love God.*

"I would love to come to New York to see you! I haven't had the chance to come to the east coast yet and maybe you could show me around?" Cory asked me curiously as we were talking over the phone later that evening.

"I would love for you to come! I just moved; it's perfect timing!" I said.

"Okay. How about next week? I will book my flight for early Friday morning since it's a time difference here in Seattle. I can take you out to dinner that evening!" Cory said excitedly.

"That sounds great! Seattle! Seattle, Washington? That's where you live now?" I asked full of excitement.

"Yeah! It's beautiful here too! You would like it," Cory said. It seemed to me he had this planned out already; knowing Cory he most likely did. Since I was a detective now my schedule is a little flexible and Fridays are lighter days; it was right on time.

"Okay, I'll see you soon! Is it alright if we could still talk until then?" he asked.

"Oh yes! We'll talk, hun!" I said to him sweetly. From that evening leading up to our dinner date we talked every day and every night.

Ring…Ring.

"Hello, handsome," I answered softly.

"Hello, gorgeous, I made it in! I'll be there to pick you up at 8:00 pm; is that okay?" he asked.

"Sounds good! You have the directions to get to my place, right?" I asked him.

"Yes, darling!" he said in an English accent. We both laughed.

"Okay, see you soon!" I said.

"Alright, love," Cory said with a sexy voice. I was happy I didn't have to work today and everything was already done. I went to get a French tip manicure and pedicure, went to the salon to get my hair done; I had it put into a classic French roll. I headed to Sacks Fifth Avenue to find the perfect dress for the evening. I could've shopped last week but I may have changed my mind in between time and with going now it has to be a final decision. It didn't take me long to find what I was looking for; I already had a vision on what I wanted to wear. I chose an emerald green silk, scooped neck, mid sleeve, knee length backless dress. I accessorized the dress with peacock feather rhinestone dangle earrings. A simple emerald green Swarovski crystal bracelet, a gold and rhinestone mini clutch purse. Gold strapped around the ankle pep toe shoes with a thin stiletto heel. My make-up was simple; a little powder and eyeliner under my eyes and on top of my eyelids. Mascara, a hint of emerald green and a pinch of gold eye shadow around the inside of my eyes, with a lite splash of my favorite MAC gold lip-gloss. To top everything off I picked up my vintage perfume bottle my mother gave me filled with COCO Channel Mademoiselle perfume and gently sprayed my pressure points; both my wrist and neck. I looked at the finished product in the mirror and said to myself out loud, '*I'M A BAD MAMA JAMA!*'

Ring…Ring.

My heart skipped a beat as I answered the phone. "Hello!" I said with a sexy grin.

"I'm outside baby!" he said. This is it! I get to see Cory for the first time in thirteen years!

"Here I come," I said shyly. I took my time to walk down the stairs and when I opened the door, there he was! Lord, help me Jesus Christ of Heaven and Earth; Cory was already handsome but now with age he is the most beautiful thing I've ever laid my eyes on. He had on a jet-black suit, with a black dress shirt with a few buttons open. To top it off he had some expensive black Stacy Adams shoes that had a gold trim around them. Cory had grown a goatee mustache that was manicured to his face along with a perfect line up with waves; his hair is still jet-black.

His skin glowed like he stepped out of Heaven; beholding this shape of a man almost made me paralyzed. In a trance for a moment; I felt as if I was moving in slow motion. His blazer swayed from the cool evening breeze as he started walking toward me. I could smell him the closer he came; the smell of Creed cologne. I almost passed out as soon as he smiled. When he was close enough, he looked at me deep in the eyes, took my hand and kissed it. He turned me around to get a full 360-degree view. We hugged each other for a good five minutes. To feel his body on mine felt right; we complimented each other beautifully. He took my hand and walked me to the Mercedes Benz stretch limo; I was in awe. The ride was smooth; as I looked out the window, I thought to myself, '*As long as I've lived in New York I haven't seen it like this before*.' You don't really need a car here; although, I still have one. Sometimes I would take a cab or the train; I haven't had the chance to experience the city in a luxury car and it was magical. I felt special, as a Queen! We laughed and hugged. We didn't kiss; we just looked at each other in the eyes. Dinner was at Benson's on the rooftop. I've heard about this restaurant but I didn't have anyone special to go with; I mentioned it to him that I would like to go. '*He listened to me*,' I thought to myself when the car pulled up to the door; it made me feel heard.

When the host took us to our table, we had the most breathtaking view. I could see almost all of New York with the evening city lights and in the distance a view of the Statue of Liberty. "It's truly amazing that we get to have this opportunity once more to be in each other's company," Cory said.

"I know. God is something else!" I said.

"Yes. He is!" Cory said.

"Why now after all this time?" I asked before the waiter came. I started deep into his eyes as if I was staring into his soul; I continued. "I wanted to wait until we saw each other in person to ask you this question."

He stared back without blinking an eye and said, "Misty, you have always been the one. We were young and had to live our lives a little bit. It was the most painful decision that I ever had to make. Breaking your heart in the process messed me up but I knew it had to be done. I didn't want to hurt you or hold you back from pursuing your dreams. Now that you have accomplished your dream and have become who God created you to be, I felt drawn to find you! That's why now!" he answered sincerely.

"You were never far from my mind but I had to grow up first. So, I got married and although she was a lovely lady, we were both incompatible. We rushed our relationship. She wanted to have children right away; I did too but not that soon until we grew more in our marriage. I admit I made selfish choices and would shut her out emotionally. The truth is; we weren't ready for each other! With time, mental space and having to work on myself; I feel I can be the man God will be pleased with and also be the man for you, Misty."

As a tear rolled down my face I was in a daze. *'Could this really be happening to me right now!'* I thought to myself. Any woman would want for the man of her dreams to confess how he feels about her.

Yes, it takes time for a man/woman to mature and say; I've made mistakes, I've learned and I'm here! Right in front of you putting my heart in your hand! I was overwhelmed with pure joy. I finally said with love, "I don't know what to say. I'm speechless! I respect you and everything you said to me and I'm so grateful that this moment has come for us." He wiped the single tear from my cheek; he held and caressed my chin with his hand. I was looking directly at his eyes they were filled with flames and he was dead serious. The waitress came and Cory ordered the top of the line champagne.

As we lifted our crystal glass flutes to the sky for a toast, he held my hand and said, "TO US!"

"Would you like to come up and see my new place?" I asked Cory when the limo rolled up to my apartment.

"I would be honored, my lady!" he said. Once we got inside and made our selves comfortable, he wanted to see my badge. I went to go get it from my dresser and when I came out the bedroom to show him, he grabbed me by the waist and kissed me desperately. I kissed him back with just as much passion; fire and desire. He picked me up and took me to my room. On this night I lost my virginity to Cory kinsmen.

I called Elaine after Cory left. "Hey, Elaine, what's up?"

"GIRLL…how did everything go? I can't believe you and Cory are back together!" Elaine said over the phone.

"Me too! I still can't believe it myself! I have something to tell you; I haven't told anyone!" I said to her.

"WHAT? What are you hiding?"—She pauses for a minute and then realizes what it is—"OOOHHH! YOU AND CORY ARE DOING THE NASTY!" she says as she then recognizes it's Misty's first time! "OH MY GOD! You lost your virginity! I know you have been waiting but YOU DID IT!" Elaine said stunned.

"Yes, and it's been amazing; something I've never felt before!" I said anxiously.

"So, where do you guys go from here?" Elaine asked.

"I don't know but what I know for sure is that he's the only man for me and has always been!" I answered.

"I hear you, Mist! You and Cory belong together I knew that already! Don't let it go on any longer that way 'cause you know you're living for the Lord! How's Qena doing?" Elaine asked.

"You're right and I'll get my head together! She's good! I'll let her know you asked about her. Don't you have her number? Call her sometimes!" I said laughing.

"You're right! DUH!" Elaine laughs then turns serious and says, "Make sure you and Cory come to an understanding; it's really important that you do."

"You're right, sis; I will!"

"I'm happy for you, Misty, and I believe he's the one for you too. I remember you mentioning him along with Ocean but I knew he was the one you had in your heart,"

Qena said. I called her after I got off the phone with Elaine to check in and let her know how everything went.

"The time we spent was so special and we ended up sleeping together. I lost my virginity to him!" I told Qena.

"WOW, I didn't know you were still a virgin, Mist, but that's wonderful that you were able to give your precious flower to someone you trust. I kind of figured you were waiting for marriage by the way you carried yourself and your faith in God. I didn't want to assume you were sexually involved. Remember your morals; you were waiting for a reason," Qena said.

"Yeah, Q! You're right and I hear you!" I said to Qena.

"How's Elaine doing? I know she was excited!" Qena said.

"Yeah, she was!" I said laughing. "She also said the same thing as you; reminding me of my morals and staying focused. Ummm. Don't you have her number? I sound like a broken record; I just told her the same thing." I said laughing.

"Oh yeah, I do! Mist, you know I don't have many friends; you and now Elaine is what I call friends. I'll give her a call as soon as I hang up with you!" Qena said.

"Yes! You should!" I said as we were both laughing!

For the past three months it's been a whirlwind. Cory and I are still seeing and sleeping with one another. On Valentine's Day when I came home from a long day at work, I opened the door to my apartment; I saw dozens upon dozens of sunflowers! I was so surprised; it warmed my heart to see this! I saw a note at the bottom of the flowers on my famous coffee table and when I opened it; it said, "*Come and see me!*" There was a ticket attached to Seattle, WA leaving in about two hours! It was already 3:00 pm my time and I'm three hours ahead of him. I had to make a dash for it to get my things ready and call in for work for the next three days; I used some of my sick time. There was another surprise; a driver in a Lincoln town car was waiting to take me to the airport when I stepped outside the door! I thought to myself. '*I'm just too threw with Mr. Cory!*' I laughed inside. I made it in a nick of time and landed at around 7:45 pm Seattle time.

When I got off the plane and went outside, there was a driver waiting with a sign and my name was on it. I followed him to a Mercedes stretch limo like the one Cory came to pick me up in on our first date. Once I walked up to the door he got out! He grabbed and picked me up off the ground and was spinning us around as we laughed carelessly! He put me down, looked me in the eyes and said, "Happy Valentine's Day, my love!" Then he kissed me.

Seattle is gorgeous! The air is crisp and clear. I could drink water from the faucet because it's already purified! Cory told me it rains a lot here which is why the air is so breathable; inhaling it was indeed a breath of fresh air! The lush green pastures and the picture-perfect scenery made it look like an oil painting. We went to the monuments; the Space Needle, Pike Place Public market where I saw the men tossing the fish whenever someone ordered. It's their routine and they would pass the fish all around to everyone behind the counter! We ate some of the best seafood I've ever eaten on this side of Heaven. We walked around the market and I got some magnets, key rings and a piggy bank! We went to Mount Rainier and the view was astounding! Seattle is definitely a place to come and get away from all the hustle and bustle in New York. It seemed more like a retirement city; nevertheless it's remarkable.

Cory and I haven't attended church since we've been together. I admit I've been in my own little world and haven't been going as much as I should have. I let him know that we were going to church this Sunday and he agreed since he grew up in the church as well. The service was beautiful; I had the chance to introduce Cory to my pastor and first lady after service was over.

"Pastor Jeremiah Hughes and First Lady Ava Hughes, this is my boyfriend Cory," I said.

"Hello, Pastor Jeremiah and First lady Ava Hughes," Cory said as he reached out his hand and pastor shook it and embraced him; he shook Mrs. Hughes hand gently and she hugged him.

"Thank you for coming! It's so good to see you, Misty, and this nice young man!" Mrs. Hughes said with love.

"Yes, ma'am, the pleasure is mine! The service was amazing, pastor; you have a beautiful church," Cory said.

"Thanks, Cory, we appreciate you coming! We look forward to hosting a wedding soon with the both of you," Pastor Hughes said with love and sincerity.

"Yes, sir, that would be great but not anytime soon," Cory said in a lazy tone. I had to keep myself together as I felt a knot in my stomach. I played it off and smiled.

"Well don't wait too long. Sister Misty is a wonderful person with a beautiful soul. A great citizen to our community and she loves the Lord! You'll know when you're ready; we wish you all the best!" pastor said. I stood in silence and kept smiling to hide from the embarrassment.

"Thank you, pastor, for your gracious compliments; it means a lot," I said to Pastor Hughes all the while still processing what I heard "*No time soon!*"

"What's wrong with you? You've been quiet the whole ride home!" Cory asked me when we walked into my apartment. I had to get my thoughts in order before I said anything and not let my emotions get the best of me.

"What did you mean by saying, no time soon, Cory?" I asked with an attitude.

"What are you talking about?" he asked me.

"So, we have amnesia now? What you said to the pastor when he asked about us taking the next step to marriage?" I asked him.

"Baby, you know I was divorced and I'm not trying to go that route right now!" he said.

"That was five years ago, Cory! What are we doing? How long do you think this is going to keep happening?" I asked with fury.

"We're together and I like how things are now! I'm not sure if I want to get married again but I want to be with you!" he answered calmly and genuinely.

I liked that about him he's a laid-back type of guy while I'm the firecracker. I learn to match my tone with his; I don't want to raise my voice. We're both adults, we'll handle this as such but I don't like what I'm hearing and I was getting upset. "This is my fault! I got caught up with you and I should've let you know that I want to get married in the future. I haven't been with anyone sexually and I wanted to save myself for my husband. I know what I want and I will not continue sleeping with you until you figure out what *YOU* really want! I don't want to be in a dead-end relationship. I've waited too long and I know what I deserve Cory. I understand where you are and why you would want to put off that commitment. I'm not rushing you; I'm just letting you know where I'm coming from. I believe it's best we don't see each other for a while," I said.

"Baby, you know I love you and I'm with you now is that not good enough?" he said while starting to get agitated. "If you want to take a break, fine but don't believe for one second that I would drag you to a dead-end relationship. That was never my intentions!" he said with fury and passion. He left an hour later.

My spirit knew this was wrong. We were having sexual relations without being married. I asked the Lord for forgiveness for being selfish and not blaming anyone but myself. I'm human; I sinned but I have repented and will try my best to past the next test.

***

For two weeks we didn't speak to each other and it was driving me crazy! I threw myself into work to take my mind off of him but no matter what he was there. A couple of days later when I went to work, I saw a vase of sunflowers on my desk and my heart became warm. I took the note off the vase and it said, "*I miss you! I want to speak with you today. Call me when you get home. I love you, baby!*" My smile was so big and wide you could see my wisdom teeth. I couldn't wait to get home to call him! As I was walking up the stairs to my apartment, there he was at the door waiting. I almost fell down the stairs in shock! I ran up to him and cried. We hugged and kissed.

"Baby, I don't want to live without you, we don't have to have sex; that's not what our relationship is about. I prayed and asked the Lord to forgive me for I couldn't help myself being with you. I should've waited. The Lord is first in our relationship and He will lead us in the way we should go!" Cory said wholeheartedly.

"I don't want to live without you either and yes God is first! We can do it with His help. We'll make it!" I said.

Cory and I didn't sleep in the same bed nor did he spend the night at my apartment for five months. He would get a hotel room when he would visit and I would do the same when I went to Seattle.

***

Ring…Ring.

"Hello!" I said.

"Baby girl, how are you?" my dad asked happily over the phone. I haven't heard him this chipper in quite some time.

"Hey, Daddy! I'm well, how are you?" I asked happily.

"I'm doing fine, baby!" he said.

"How's Mom?" I asked.

"She's doing pretty good!" he said.

"That's great!" I said. No matter what was going on between Cory and I; I still went to go see about my mother and put in the time so that my father could get some rest.

"Baby girl, I want you to come home! It's no emergency; your mother and I have something special for you!" he said excitedly.

"Okay, well when should I come?" I asked.

"Come this weekend?" my dad said.

"THIS WEEKEND! Oh, Dad! This latest case has been kicking my butt—" I breathed in—"I'll see what I can do. I love you! Tell Mom, I love her too!"

"I will! Love you too, baby!" my dad said.

I'm so grateful to my team because they have been very supportive throughout everything with my family and I was able to pull away for two days.

I flew back home to North Carolina Friday afternoon and when I made it to the house that evening to my surprise Cory was there! I hugged and kissed him. I went to my bedroom and took a shower and got dressed. I put on a pink floral maxi dress with spaghetti straps. It was a warm evening and my mother was looking great! The chemo was helping! When I walked down the stairs, it felt like old times again. My mom cooked a wonderful meal. She made a pot roast; with collard greens, mashed potatoes and gravy, salad, bread rolls and a pitcher of freshly squeezed lemonade from our lemon tree in the backyard. For dessert was a homemade lemon meringue pie. My mother had the formal table set up with a beautiful crisp white lace table cloth, her best china, the gold and crystal candelabras were out with white candles that were lit. It was fabulous; I can't say it enough my mother sure is a class act indeed!

Everyone was waiting for me. We sat down to our seats at the table; my father and mother across from Cory and I. My father wanted Cory to pray. *"Dear Lord thank you for this food we are about to receive for the blessed healed hands and body that prepared it." We thank you for this gathering and celebrating true family. "In Jesus name Amen!"* I was confused because I didn't know what was happening.

"What's the occasion?" I asked.

"Well, first I wanted to tell you that Dr. Osikia called and said that the cancer is in remission!" my mom said.

"OH MY GOD! HALLELUJAH!" I hollered with my hands up! I could see my mom gaining weight; she was starting to look and feel like herself slowly but surely! We all clapped and thanked the Lord for His healing of my mom. Then Daddy stood up to say something.

"I have a special announcement as well but I would like for Cory to do the honors." As he sat down, Cory stood up next to me but then he got down on one knee and took my

136

hand! I started to hyperventilate! I was so overwhelmed; I didn't know what to do! Then Cory began speaking.

"I've been in love with you since the day I met you. I've always known you were the one for me. There's nothing in this world that I can't go through with you by my side. Your faith is Godly, your strength is unbreakable and I need you to walk with me all the days of my life until the day I die! Misty Joyce Rivers, will you marry me?" I'm balling my eyes out and my parents are crying as well.

I managed to say a strong "YES, CORY! YES!"

When he opened the box to the ring, I gasped. It was my mother's ring! "Mommy, it's your ring!" I said crying.

"Yes, baby, for our 30th anniversary your father gave me this ring!" She showed it to me; it was amazing, a 3-karat Emerald cut diamond ring.

"He gave it to me a week ago! I said to your father that I'm going to give you the first ring. I only have one daughter and she may need it one day! Then Cory called us not to long afterward and asked us for your hand in marriage. It was impeccable timing; the Lord was arranging everything. He wanted all of us to be here but sadly your brother couldn't make it; he knew and promised us not to tell you!" my mother said filled with joy and happiness.

"WOW! He sure didn't! I love that brother of mines! Oh, Mommy, it looks beautiful as when you were wearing it!" I said while stargazing at the ring. When he slipped it onto my finger, I noticed something. "Ooohh, the diamond is bigger!" I said. I turned to look over at her and she winked at me! Together as a family we laughed, danced and talked all night long with Cory right by my side.

A couple of months later my brother finally graduated with his master's degree. Master of Science in engineering from UCLA in California it was great! I've been to California to visit my bro before and I loved the beaches there. I told Cory we should get married on the beach in California; he thought it was a cool idea since we had been planning the wedding and couldn't make up our minds about a venue. We didn't live together; he still lived in Seattle and I was in New York. We agreed once we were married that we would live in New York then move within a few years.

On May 1, 2012 Cory and I were getting married. I had one maid of honor Elaine. A maid of honor is an unwed woman and I had a matron of honor Qena. Qena is married so she's considered a matron of honor. Both of them wore yellow flowy tea length dresses; Qena's was off the shoulders with mid length sleeves while Elaine's had a sweetheart neckline with mid length sleeves as well. Their hair was pinned up in Shirley Temple curls, with a mother of pearl necklace, earrings and bracelet set courtesy of the bride! They would carry a beautiful bouquet of sunflowers, white calla lilies, yellow and white roses. Two flower girls who were my little cousins that were dressed in white baby doll dress with a bow on the back and ring bearer, which was also a little boy relative. Then finally the best man and groomsmen, who was Cory's good friend Basse from high school and my brother; they wore black tuxedos while Cory wore an all-white one. Ahmad was so happy he was paired up with Qena to walk down the aisle! My mother looked ravishing; she glowed in a gold dress. Her hair was short because of the chemo treatment; our family beautician cut and lined it up in a beautiful becoming style. It fit her face to a tee. Cory's grandmother Mrs. Green was able to make it. She was in a wheelchair but she was there! We made sure to incorporate a walkway on top of the sand specifically for her. She looked beautiful with a yellow sundress and her hair was pulled up in a neat classic bun. My dress was handmade by my mother and I. The dress was Cinderella style tea length, with a corset's waist, sweetheart neckline and mid length sleeves. The material was light as a feather, with crystal stones and pearl beading all over on the waist, around the sweetheart line and sleeves. My hair was down with soft loose curls and I wore my mother's veil. It was in immaculate condition; we got it cleaned and added a few stones.

When it was time to walk me down the aisle, my father and I were silent. We were very relaxed; he looked dapper in his tuxedo. I was expecting Dad to be a nervous wreck but he surprised me. He was prepared and new ultimately that this day would come. There was a moment right on cue were we both turned and locked eyes with one another. I could see the joy of the Lord in his eyes; something I couldn't explain. I've never until this moment had the honor to experience it. I wasn't mature enough to neither appreciate nor understand this love and I may never fully grasp the totality if it. It's no ordinary love that I was beholding it felt as if God looked at His Son Jesus Christ with acceptance and was well pleased. I almost broke down from being overwhelmed. It was powerful. My father is my pillar of strength but my Heavenly Father is the *source* of my strength. There's nothing more I could ever ask for in this world than to have a father's love.

Chapter 8
The Little Things

Charlie Winston Baker was born on March 20, 1979 in Fayetteville, North Carolina. He grew up in a stable upbringing with his parents Frances and Bobby Baker. He's 6'2", light skinned, slim with broad shoulders; with light brown eyes and a crooked smile. Average looking guy to some but would be extremely handsome to most. He was a football player in high school, confident; slightly arrogant with a good sense of humor. Charlie had a few friends in high school but kept to himself; he has a good relationship with his mother and father. Most guys follow into their father's footsteps but Charlie took a different path. He became a police officer, moved to New York and pursued a different life. Charlie has some unfinished business and is holding a dark secret. He's now working at the same precinct as Misty. Charlie knows Misty from high school; he found her attractive but they never interacted with one another.

Charlie would see Misty at the homecoming games; some of his football teammates would talk about getting with her. He would see Misty around campus and when Cory would pick her up from school.

The year is 2012 in the middle of spring. We see Capt. Joshua's office at the precinct. Charlie is inside the captain's office where he has received some good news.

"Captain, I want to thank you for welcoming me here; this is a tuff station to get into!" Charlie said with pride.

"Well, Detective Charlie, you earned it! You should be proud of yourself!" Capt. Joshua said while congratulating him. Charlie nods and smiles while shaking Capt. Joshua's hand.

Fifteen years earlier…in the evening around 9:30 pm; Charlie has come home from football practice and is in the kitchen sitting at the table eating a late dinner from the plate his mother left for him. He's dressed for bed when Frances Baker his mother comes in and sits down next to him. Frances had a tough life growing up. She was a runaway; had a bad attitude but learned to tame it when she got older. Frances is a recovered drug addicted and has been clean since becoming a mother to her only child. She has that old-time glamor look; a unique beauty. 5'2", light skinned, with long brown wavy hair and light brown eyes; Charlie looks exactly like her.

"Charlie, there is something important I need to discuss with you before you graduate from high school," Frances said nervously. Charlie ate the last bite of his hamburger and then focused his attention on his mother.

"Before I met your father, I was with another man. I met him in the streets when I ran away from home at seventeen years old. He was much older than I; He was twenty-five.

142

We would steal from people; I would drive the getaway car when he would rob houses or stores. We both did drugs together: that's actually how I got started. You knew I did drugs but I never told you how it began. We were young, wild and carefree. We were inseparable. He looked after me. I had no idea what love was because I didn't get any at home; I thought he loved me or so what I *thought* was love! I had gotten pregnant at eighteen and I wanted to change my life. I didn't want to end up like my folks who were both alcoholics."

Charlie sat and listened; he knew were this was going. He had a bad temper; once his blood gets boiling the beast comes out! Frances has had to put him into therapy sessions when he was younger to control his problem. When he was thirteen years old, he had an incident in middle school. Charlie felt that his teacher embarrassed him in front of the students when she called him out for not paying attention. After class ended everyone left and he walked right up to the teacher and spit in her face!

For three years he went to therapy to learn how to control his anger issues. Now, as he's sitting here with his mother telling him about this other man; the pieces are starting to come together. Frances continued, "We were hanging on by a thread money wise. I told him we should put this life behind us and start fresh but he couldn't let go of his demons. I left your father when you were two months old. I couldn't take it anymore; I wanted to change for *you!* I didn't hear from him again. We loved each other; he just didn't have the tools to turn his life around for *us!* I worked odd jobs and went back to school at a community college. I had a friend of mine whose family owned a day care." Ms.

Esther would watch you sometimes even when I couldn't afford to pay her; that was a true blessing! I met Bobby when you were eight months old at a coffee shop I was working at. We got married a year later, moved away and we've been together ever since. I tried to stay in contact with Ms. Esther and my friend Bella once we moved but I dropped my phone in a puddle and lost all of my contacts. I even went back to the day care to find them; sadly Ms. Esther passed away and the family sold the business.

"One morning after your father left for work and you were at school; I believe you were seven at the time—" Frances pauses for a moment then breathes. She is starting to cry, what she's getting ready to say is really hard and a bomb is about to drop on Charlie—"I was watching the news about a man on the run for murdering two police officers and fled the state. When I saw the drawing of the man, I knew it was him! I made sure to protect you from all of that madness and never mentioned it until now! Bobby knows because I wanted to be honest with him about my past. I was grateful he understood to leave the decision to me; to let you know the truth about who your real father is."

By this time Frances was gently crying. With a little bit of anger and disappointment in his voice Charlie asked, "What's his name, Mama?"

Frances put her hands over her face; she couldn't even look at him. Then she lifted her head out of her hands; looked at him in the eyes and said, "Winston. Winston Poe!" Charlie recognizing that his middle name is in fact Winston and it was his real fathers name all along!

"I'm so sorry, baby! I love you so much; you are my life and I-I just didn't know how to tell you!" Frances said sobbing. Charlie is really dumfounded! Devastated! He knew it was coming as the story was unfolding but to actually confirm his father is a murderer was almost unbearable. He hugged his mother having some type of compassion toward her as she continued weeping on her son's shoulder. He couldn't blame her for keeping this secret but was still very hurtful. Charlie somehow understood her reasons to wait until he was able to comprehend what she had to tell him later on in life.

Men are taught not to show emotions and Charlie was no exception. He tried hard not to show anything; it didn't work and a single tear fell down his face. Bobby his stepfather was strict; he was a Marine in the army. He's an Alpha male through and through. Bobby didn't abuse Charlie but he didn't take any mess! Bobby Baker is husky, 6'0", dark skinned, jet-black hair, high cheekbones with a sly grin. On a nice summer day; Bobby came into a coffee shop. He doesn't drink coffee but he saw Frances working there, decided to come in and try his first cup. He was trying to impress Frances to take her out on a date. It worked; when she told him that she had a son he welcomed her. Bobby is all Charlie knows as a father. He never once felt like Bobby wasn't his real father; they had their ups and downs as any family does especially when Charlie was testing his parents with his behavior but Bobby wouldn't let him go too far off the deep end and stayed by his side.

Instead of the discipline that Booby was used to as a kid Frances convinced him to send Charlie to therapy. Bobby was very involved in Charlie's life and was an excellent provider; he lacked affection because he never had it. His idea of affection is a handshake; he barely hugged. Bobby and Frances never had any children together. Bobby's daughter Grace he had with his ex-girlfriend died of SIDS (sudden infant death syndrome) when she was two months old. They broke up and three years later he met Frances.

"Mama, it's going to be alright. Please go and get some rest; we all needed it!" Charlie said calmly.

After she collected herself and started to walk out the kitchen, she turned to him and said, "Bobby insisted that I tell you. If it weren't for him, I would've been too ashamed! I would've gone to my grave with this secret. I'm so glad you know the truth," Frances said relieved.

Charlie looked at his mother with so many emotions he had no idea he could possibly feel. He nodded and said, "I'm glad you told me and mama; I'm going to look for my father! It may not be for a while but I am going to find him someday!"

Frances looked at her son; she could see Winston in his eyes. "You're a young man now and can make your own decisions, son. I know you'll do the right thing; be wise. Please, please be careful! If something were to happen to you, I don't know what I would do. You're all I have and I thank your father for giving me *you!*" Frances said peacefully and gave him a loving look as she walked out the kitchen. Charlie was left alone with his thoughts.

Charlie attended Michigan State University and began his long search for his fugitive father. He went to the libraries and searched for all the newspaper articles. While reading the articles he made sure to make a mental note of the officers that were on the scene: Officer Warren Tate, Sergeant Anita Lopez, Detective Andrew Rivers and Detective John Hill. As he kept reading it said: Detectives Andrew Rivers and John Hill were later assigned to the case. When Charlie saw the drawing of Winston for the very first time, he was overcome with disbelief; he was looking right into his own eyes. It was disturbing and made him feel sick to his stomach. Although, the drawing was old the resemblance was striking. Winston was brown skinned, with dark brown eyes, sinewy frame, 6'2" and 140 pounds. He may have his mother's complexion but seeing Winston and Charlie's profile they were definitely related. He searched the computer engines and even went so far to call the police station in Fayetteville. He couldn't get any answers because till this day the case remained opened. *"The only way I can get those files is for me to join the police force!"* he said to himself when he hung up the phone from talking to the North Carolina police department.

The night Charlie graduated from college Frances and Bobby hosted a party in their home. "I would like to make an announcement!" Charlie said as he stood up from the dinner table facing his family, aunts, uncles and handful of cousins. "I've decided; I'm going to join the police force! Yes, I have a degree in business management but I feel that I'm lead to be a police officer!" Frances's was livid; her face turned a slight shade of crimson red. Bobby was sitting next to her when he caught her disappointment and rubbed Frances back in support. They looked up at Charlie with confusion in their eyes; Frances had to calm herself down. She didn't want to embarrass Charlie for not agreeing with his decision; she held her peace and accepted it.

Within the next three years Charlie becomes a policeman in Fayetteville and could finally get his hands on the unauthorized files of his father's crime. Upon looking through the files to his surprise he finds out that Winston's last sighting was in Mexico City. At that moment Charlie decides to back off the search. He feels apprehensive on going to Mexico City and wasn't as ready as he thought he was. Charlie had to figure out a plan first and decided that he would move to New York to be closer to Mexico City. He wanted to gain more experience by going up in ranks and hopefully having some pull into helping his father.

Two years later in 2006 Charlie moved to New York and worked at the 23rd division for six years. Present day. 2012. He's transferred from the 23rd to the 54th division precinct; he has been keeping the case and Winston being his father a secret for fifteen years! Charlie is shaking hands with Capt. Joshua and he's quite fond of Charlie.

"Captain, I haven't used any of my vacation time in three years! I've been a workaholic and I would like to use it now!" Charlie asked.

He could feel in his spirit the time was now or never. "Charlie, you got it! Your record is exceptional! You've only been here a week and done more work than a guy who's been here for years already! Go and enjoy yourself, Son!" Capt. Joshua said warmly.

Charlie booked the next flight to Mexico City! He didn't care if he had to search every corner. It was going to be an extremely hard road but whatever it took to get to the truth; he walked around with the photo of Winston.

"Excuse me! Have you seen this man?" Charlie asked an older Hispanic gentleman. He shook his head no. He went to the stores, bars, clubs, young and old, men, women and children; all nodded in a no gesture. Later that night in his hotel room as he was studying the file when he grew frustrated, the phone rang!

Ring…Ring.

"Hello! Hey, Dad!" Charlie said.

"Hey, Son! How's it going?" Bobby asked.

"I knew it would be a task but I'm not giving up!" Charlie said.

"I know that we don't talk much because you've been so consumed in trying to find your father. I wanted to let you know that I believe what your doing is the most courageous thing I've ever seen. Having the guts to go hand and foot in finding your roots. I've never had to experience that and I'm proud of you, Son!" Bobby said genuinely. Charlie could hardly breathe; he was taking in every word his father said. Bobby never told him he was proud of him. Only a head nod of approval or a handshake with a light hug came very far in between. Hearing this made him feel loved for the first time by a *father*.

Charlie was silent for a moment. "Thanks, Dad! I appreciate it!" he said with a warm smile; he could feel the effect of Bobby's kindness in his soul.

"I'll let you go! Your mother and I are going out to the movies! We'll talk soon!"

"Bye, Son," Bobby said with love.

"Bye, Dad!" After he hung up the phone, he decided to step out for some air on his hotel room terrace; he hasn't had the chance to take in the beautiful site. As Charlie stood outside; he looked up at the moonlight sky and saw a full moon over the dark waters of the ocean. He closed his eyes and didn't think about anything; only feeling the warm breeze taking over him.

Charlie got on his knees and started to pray. *"Oh God, Father in Heaven! I'm so sorry for ignoring you for the past 15 years! I was angry with you for allowing me to have a father who had done unforgivable acts but just like you have forgiven me. I forgive him too. I need your help father in helping me finish this mission. I can't do it without you! Thank you, Lord! Amen!"* That night Charlie had the best sleep he's ever had.

TAP! TAP! TAP! "HOUSEKEEPING?"

Charlie woke up frantic but calm down once he realized it wasn't a bad dream. He slept long and hard; he was even sweating a little bit. "Give me a few minutes and then you can come in!" Charlie answered. Once he got out of bed, he put his robe on and opened the door. He saw the little elderly lady a few doors down and waved for her to come back.

"Hello! I would like some towels please and could you empty the trash?"

As she was walking back toward him, she said, "Si senor." When she looked up at him, she gasped. "OH MY GOD!" Her English was broken but she managed to get some words out. "You looka like ths man I see years ago at a hotel I used to work at! I clean room for him and I see that he was ths man on the news! I didn't react; I clean room for him and he was nice. He told me not to be a-fraid; he needs someone to talk to! He wouldn't let anyone else clean room for him; expect me! He was there for seis months; six months! We became friends. I made sure that none of my co-workers came to the area where I cleaned for him," the lady said with excitement.

Charlie was in complete shock of what he heard; he ran and grabbed the photo from his table.

"Is this the man?" Charlie asked anxiously.

She looked intensely at the photo and without a shadow of a doubt... "SI! YES! That's him!" the lady said. So many questions went to his head he didn't know what to ask first!

"What's your name? Where is he? When was the last time you saw him?" Charlie asked frantically.

"My name Coco! I not sure; the last time we spoke was eight years ago and he say he was going back home! He moved not to fa from here about 30 minutes away on Domingo Street! He lived in the back of a house; thas all I kno! His name is Rico Vargas!" Charlie had to sit down; he felt his stomach starting to feel queasy. *This is an answered prayer!* He couldn't help but to think this was all a dream.

He waited for so long and now everything has hit him all at once! All he could do was stare at Coco.

He waited a moment and said, "I'm his son! I'm trying to find him! Thank you so much!" Charlie said whole-heartily. Coco was overjoyed; hugged and cried in his arms. He hugged her back gently and full of gratitude.

"You look like him! I wouldn't ever forget his face!" Coco said sincerely.

"Do you still have the address?"

Charlie went out into the terrace again; this time it was in the afternoon. He's standing there; paper in hand with the address Coco gave: 9311 Domingo Street apt 2 back. Charlie wasn't raised with a church background. His mom and dad went every so often but it didn't go any further. One thing his mom did teach him when he was little was to pray. Charlie knows at this moment he needs God's hand of guidance before going to meet his father. He bowed down on his knees once more out on the terrace, laid his head down and began.

"God Almighty! Forgive me! Help me get through this; I need you! I don't know what to do? I've been trying to do this alone and I can't. I recognize what you have done for me. Not with finding my earthly father but you being here every step of the way! I don't know Jesus but I want to know Him! Please continue to be a guiding force and help me to do what's right. I pray for Winston Poe. Lord, help him; give him the mind to turn himself in. Thank you, Lord. Thank God. Amen!"

Later that evening Charlie pulled up in front of an old dilapidated house; he had butterflies in his stomach. He got out the car and walked to the back where it looked like a mini house. It seemed as if someone still lived there; the light was on and he could hear a radio playing inside. He looked at the address on the paper again 9311 and looked up at the house; the numbers matched. He took a deep breath and knocked twice. *TAP! TAP!* No one came to the door. He waited and knocked again. *TAP! TAP!* No answer. As he turned to walk away the door creaked open slightly.

Hearing the sound Charlie turned around and walked back to the slightly open door; he slowly opened it. There was a man sitting in a chair in the living room listening to the radio. Inside the house was dim and small; there were newspapers, shoes and books around. Borderline hording. It smelled like he had finished cooking some chili with spices and peppers. It was warm and surprisingly inviting. Charlie walked up half way into the living room where Winston was sitting in his chair to get a really good look at him. There he was face to face with his father.

"Hello, Son!" Winston said quietly. Charlie was astonished. He couldn't believe he was looking in the eyes of his real father; what he saw in them was full of deceit, darkness and regret. Charlie is staring at him unable to say a word; still standing in front of him.

"You don't think I would recognize my only son! I saw you way before I came to Mexico City. I laid low for a while. I slept in farm sheds, abandoned buildings; park benches and with the homeless. I couldn't leave until I saw you grow up some. I saw your mother with you; taking you to day care, kindergarten, and elementary school. I left not long after," Winston said. Charlie finally managed to speak.

"You saw us struggling and didn't bother to help?"

"What could I do? I didn't want to put your mother through any more hell that I had already caused—"

"You are already did enough by killing two people let alone two policemen! What were you thinking? Oh! You weren't because you were only thinking of yourself and your devious ways!" Charlie said as he interrupted Winston.

"No, Son! I was young, destructive and on drugs; your mother didn't know that. She thought I quit using but I had a secret habit. I didn't know anything else but a life of crime!" Winston said sincerely. Charlie looked at his father in disgust. He had to try and understand his father's point of view; he only knew one side to the story. Now, that he could hear from his father maybe he could start having compassion.

"Did you ever think about getting help for your demons?" Charlie asked hastily.

"I wanted to but I didn't make the effort. I felt that I was unfixable—"

"So, you gave up on yourself since that was the easiest thing to do—"

"Look I made a lot of mistakes and I didn't have anybody to raise me. I raised myself; being abandoned at birth and living from foster home to foster home. I never had a family! I didn't know how to have one let alone learn to be a man! Your mother was the best thing that ever happened to me…" Winston pauses as he thinks about Frances. He continues, "…I wanted to desperately kick my habit; try to live a good life with her but I was also greedy and wanted it all at the same time. I'd seen a couple that looked like they had money. They were making out in the driver seat of the car with the seat pulled back; not paying any attention. I robbed them and stole the car! I wasn't trying to kill anyone it just ended up in a horrific way! I can't take it back now! I'm getting older and I know I need to turn myself in but I just can't do it—"

"WHAT DO YOU MEAN YOU CAN'T DO IT?" Charlie yelled while listening to his father and trying to understand him. "You've had a lot of time to think about this." He calmed down. "Are you ready now?" Charlie asked his father intently. Winston took a moment to really think about his son's question. He has wanted to do right but the demon inside won't let him. Winston thought to himself, '*if I agree to go with my son, I will not go without a fight! I'm going to rot in prison for the rest of the time I have left! Do I really want to do this? Yeah, I'll go along with it but I got something else in mind!*'

Winston answered softly, "Seeing you makes me what to go back!"

The next day Charlie rented a car and they were headed on the road back to New York. Charlie's plan is to have Winston stay with him until he finds a great attorney to get his case in order. Although, Charlie was breaking the law by harboring a fugitive Winston is still his father and he was willing to risk everything to make it right.

Four days later Charlie is back to work from his 'vacation' and is seen talking to Terry.

"Man, did you see Kobe throw that 3-pointer shot? It was insane, man!" Terry said while sitting on top his desk talking to Charlie at the police station. Charlie and Terry are associates and they have spoken to each other in passing. Man talk.

"Kobe is cool! He's got mad skills, maybe one of the best of all time!" Charlie said as they do a high-five man handshake in agreement; as that happens Misty walks by.

"Hey, congratulations, Misty! You're going to love married life!" Terry said as he walks up to her and gives her a hug.

"Hey, thank you so much! Looking forward to it and congratulations to you, Sergeant Terry! I'm so proud of you!" Misty said with love.

"You're welcome and thanks, Mist!" Terry said while hugging Misty. After the short embrace Terry turns around an almost forgets to introduce Misty to Charlie.

"Oh yeah! This is Detective Charlie Baker he's from Fayetteville, North Carolina too!" Terry said excitedly.

"OH WOW! It's really a small world! Did you go to MLK High School?" Misty asked instinctively.

"Yeah, I did! I remember seeing you but I didn't ever approach you. There was a guy that would pick you up from school he had a nice car! Was that your boyfriend?" Charlie asked Misty being nosy.

"Yeah, he was! That's the guy I just got married too!" Misty said while laughing.

"Congratulations, that's great!" Charlie said.

"Are you changing your last name?" Terry asked Misty.

156

"We thought about it and…no. Cory doesn't mind; he knows I'll do it when I'm ready! I'll always be a *RIVERS*!" Charlie thought he was hard of hearing.

"*RIVERS!* Oh, okay that's cool! So…*Misty Rivers* is your full name?" Charlie asked in an inquiring tone.

"Yes, that's me! Misty Rivers! Well, it's nice to meet a fellow North Carolinian; I'll see you around. Nice talking to you!" Misty told Charlie and looked over and said to Terry, "And congrats again, Terry!" She walked away.

"Same to you, Mist, see you later!" Terry said.

Walking away from Terry's desk after the brief encounter Charlie couldn't believe what he heard. He thought to himself, *I've looked at that file for years and I remembered the names of the officers like the back of my hand! One of them was Detective Andrew Rivers…Misty is Andrew River's daughter!*

When Charlie got home that night, he couldn't contain himself. He had been trying to figure out a way for someone else to help him with his father's case and he has! He bolted to his desk in the living room and took out the file! As he was at his desk, he noticed something; no one was there! The apartment was an average one bedroom and there wasn't any room for anyone to hide. He would usually hear Winston in the bathroom or he would be in his room. He gave his father his room while he slept on the couch. Charlie had Winston on house arrest but that didn't seem to work! Charlie started panicking; searching everywhere. In the closets, bathroom and the outside window near the fire escape. Nothing. He then walked back to his desk and sat down trying to think about his next move. Then he saw some writing on his desk calendar it was a message from Winston: *"Catch me if you can! In North Carolina!"* Charlie felt defeated; his plans crumbled right before his eyes.

Charlie came to work early the next day with his plan b. He tried to remain calm and keep a poker face as he went to the captain and requested sick leave. Charlie knew he had the time even though he had to extend his vacation trying to get Winston in order. The captain approved; Charlie was on the next plane to Fayetteville, North Carolina.

I came back to work from my honeymoon feeling like a new woman; only because I'm married now! It was so good to see Terry! I can't actually believe I met someone who I went to high school with here but it happens; look at me and now Charlie! He seems familiar and nice.

The next morning when I got to my desk, there was an old looking file on top of all the other files I had. I was curious. I hurried up; sat down and went to work. Inside the file I read: *October 28, 1986 at 12:00 am on Holt Road in Fayetteville, North Carolina two officers were gunned down. They are identified as Officer Brian Scott and Officer Eddie Byrd. The assailant fled the scene. The next day they found an abandoned car; a 1986 burgundy Cadillac 25 miles toward the fair grounds. Forensics checked for prints and found two fingerprints around the steering wheel and they couldn't find a match at the time. Two shots were fired and hit the back window and a third shot hit the trunk. Two bullet shells were found inside in the back seat; the last shell casing was never recovered.*

The bullet shells were taken for ballistic testing and confirmed they came from a Colt .45 Revolver gun, the gun belonged to Officer Byrd. The murder weapon was found near a shallow pond not far from where the car was abandoned. It was a 9mm handgun; the serial number was H4687. The police checked the records on who bought the gun and the name Winston Poe was on record. He purchased it in North Carolina and signed that name; there was a signature on the books (receipt). Due to an eyewitness sighting they said they saw a man on October 28, 1986 around 1: 30 am go inside of the Gemini Hotel near the fair grounds. Winston used an alias Peter Mound and signed his name at 1: 45 am in the hotel's books (receipt).

As I continued to read the report it said: *Five years ago someone whose name is blacked out had the hand writing expert compare the signatures and the way the P's were signed it was a perfect match to how Winston wrote his P in* his last name. They checked the database and still hadn't found him. In 2012 that same someone who blacked out there name went and checked with advanced digital finger printing technology. They digitally took the fingerprints off of the crime scene photo from the steering wheel and found a match with a photo of Winston Poe. He was arrested three years earlier for a robbery in New Orleans, Louisiana. His prints were found in the Louisiana state police database!

WOW! Oh, my Lord! I thought to myself, 'That's why my father was so frustrated; back then they had limited resources!' With only a drawing of Winston to go on they could only do so much; looking at the actual photo of Winston after 26 years is priceless! Of course he has changed dramatically over the years but your face structure is always the same. I noticed something when I looked through the crime scene photos. I said to myself, 'These are so worn and tattered!' I reached for my magnifying glass and looked closer; I noticed there was a speck of blood on the back of the driver seat! My theory is that the third shot came through the trunk and hit Winston! They couldn't find the hole because the seat was leaned back as he was driving. The other two bullet shells were found in the back seat and third bullet casing was never found; he may possibly have a bullet wound on his back shoulder! I wonder why nobody really took that into consideration! They should've put it out there as a clue when they were on the manhunt looking for him! My father and his team were looking at the big picture; not the elements around that *made* the picture. I'm all about the details and I believe they didn't think it mattered; all of it matters even the little things! At the end of the report it said Winston was last seen in Mexico City! I can't wait to get home to call my dad but the burning question remains; who gave me this file?

Chapter 9
Faith Is the Evidence of
Things Unseen

The Bible tells us to be anxious for nothing; I knew I had to calm down and think straight. I've been handling cold cases for a while but this one was personal; I had to compose myself before I called my father. *My prayers have been answered!* All of the trials brought me to this point! I definitely couldn't see it then not until the Lord was ready to reveal part of His mighty plan. I said to myself, '*WOW! The Lord is a wonder!*' I didn't want to talk to my dad at the station because there are too many ears. I made it a point to call him when I got home!

"Missy, that's unbelievable! I really had to let this case go because there was a lot of red tape. I'm thinking maybe it's someone on the inside that knows something and isn't saying anything. I wouldn't be surprised if it were!" he said excitedly.

"That's what I need to get to the bottom of! You should've seen the condition of the photos even though they were copies; it's only by the grace of God that I was able to see anything," I said.

"Yeah, baby girl, maybe it took for a new pair of eyes to find clues; like you did!" my dad said with pride.

"Yeah, that could be true! How's Mom?" I asked. There was silence; a silence I didn't like to hear.

"The cancer came back; it's spread all over her major organs. There's nothing more they could do; the doctor gave her four weeks, Missy. She was going to tell you but since you already called, I thought I tell you." At that moment I stopped breathing for a second.

"Missy baby, are you there? Calm down; I know it's tough to hear," he said. I was actually very proud of my dad for telling me; I didn't think he would be able to do it and I admire him all the more for doing so.

"We told Ahmad today as well," he said with sadness. I remained silent.

"Your mother was going to tell you today but you called; suffice to say it worked out," he said again as he let out a nervous laugh.

"Okay, Dad. I will talk to you guys tomorrow; tell Mom I love her," I said solemnly.

"I will, she's resting now and doing okay. I love you too! Bye!"

I had to simmer down and let my emotions cool off. Finding what could be a key piece of evidence to a case that had my father almost lose everything over lies in my one hand and now the possibility of my mother's life coming to an end in another was unfathomable. My faith as I know it became a battle but the battle isn't mines it's the Lords! This is the same circumstance that happened with my grandma and now with my mom; it's come full circle. When I got off the phone, my mother's favorite scripture came to mind; *Hebrews 11:1 Now faith is the substance of things hoped for, the evidence of things unseen*. I made the decision to believe the report of the Lord and let His will be done. I can't see a way but Jesus is the way and whatever the outcome is I'll be ready. Am I fearful? A little. I'm human; however, I know the Lord doesn't give us the spirit of fear. It's a choice. I'm going to choose *not* to be fearful; be strong and of good courage. Can I break down? Absolutely! Will I retreat? No; what I will do is put on my whole armor of God because this fight has only just begun.

"Baby, I'm so sorry to hear this," Cory said to me as we lay in bed with his arms wrapped around me. I was lying on his chest and I could hear his heartbeat. I didn't want to tell him anything until we had our pillow talk; where we were both relaxed and didn't have any distractions. As soft tears rolled down my face I listened to his voice; hearing his heartbeat was comforting. "Baby, you know I'm here and I'll do everything I can to help; it's my family too and this affects me as well," he said.

"I know baby," I said softly.

"I'm very proud of you! You're closer than ever before to helping your dad finish what he started and now he could bring it to a close with your help! That's amazing!" Cory said graciously and lovingly. He lifted up my face to his and as he looked into my red wet eyes full of uncertainty he said with passion. "It's going to be alright; I'll hold your hand through it all. The Lord has me here for *you;* I'm your protector and best friend." Then he kissed me passionately.

⚲

My brother and I were upstairs talking to our mom in my parent's room when we heard my dad call us from downstairs. "Misty and Ahmad! Can you guys come down here for a minute?" We both started walking down the stairs and he motioned for us to go into the living room. We sat down on the couch across from my dad who was sitting in his chair; there were papers all around the table. It was two weeks ago from when my father told me about the cancer coming back and my mother was slowly fading away; it could be any moment now.

"I want to discuss with you your mother's final wishes, about the funeral arrangements and the things she wants you both to have," he said while fighting back tears. I started to look through the papers; then Ahmad jumped up and walked out the door to the backyard. He didn't want to hear this and neither did I. My dad looked at me and a single tear came down my face. I gave him a nod to go after Ahmad; his eyes started to water. He got up and went out to talk to him.

⚲

"Son, this is hard for everyone. I haven't spoken to you about how you feel. I've been caught up in trying to figure out how I feel. Your sister comes out with her emotions because she's in touch with them most of the time but I know it's harder for you. It was hard for me at your age and my father as well; we had to learn for ourselves how to process our emotions." Andrew said as he stood next to Ahmad lovingly. Ahmad is silent. He's standing and staring out unto the backyard of the house looking at the old tree that used to have his tree house in it when he was a kid. Reminiscing on how his mother would come out to tell him and his friends that lunch was ready. He could see her whole and healthy. He could hear her laughing while telling stories around the campfires they would have; roasting marshmallows and making s'mores. It made him feel a little better while listening to his father. Ahmad knew his dad was right. He was a mixed bag of emotions; devastated, angry, sad and hopeless.

"I understand, Dad, this is so heavy on me! I know we've had our talks and experiences together but this is on another level! I don't know, Dad—" as he took his hands out of his pockets and lifted them up—"I don't know how to deal with this!" Ahmad said as strong tears came down his face.

Andrew grabbed his son and embraced him; they cried together and he said, "I know, Son; and it's okay not to be okay. It's life unfortunately and we can't be strong all the time but we're going to be alright. I know you have spoken to your mother and I know she wants you to *try* and be strong for her. We're in this together! God won't give us more than we could bear! We'll make it through with His help! You hear me! I love you, Son!"

They were still embracing when Ahmad said, "I love you too, Dad!"

I was sitting in the living room alone while my brother and father were outside talking. I went upstairs to my parents' room and slowly opened the door. I didn't want to wake my mom up but she was already awake.

"Hey, Mommy, I thought you were sleeping?" I asked.

"I'm in and out, baby," she said in between breaths. She didn't want to let on that she was dying but I could see it in her eyes; I saw peace inside them as well. She motioned for me to come and get in the bed with her. I walked up, took off my house shoes and got in the bed with my mommy. I laid on her chest so I could hear her heartbeat. It was a cool evening as I felt a breeze come through the window. I laid on her little chest; she wrapped her arms around me as tight as she could and started rubbing the top of my head; running her fingers through my hair.

"Baby, I want you to keep going no matter what! Promise me that you will not stop!" she said with force. I felt a warm tear go down my face.

I nodded and said, "Yes, Mommy."

She took her hands; lifted my face up so I could look at her right in the eyes.

"Promise me, Missy baby, you will keep going, you're my life, my love. I've spoken to your father and brother already; they're handling this the best way they know how. It's your turn now for me to speak to you. You've been busy running around, helping to take care of me and I know you've been avoiding this. The Lord knew when the time was right to send you up here so I could speak to you," she said this with so much strength in her voice; the Holy Spirit was all over her. I stayed silent; I nodded, cried and listened to every word she said.

"Do you remember what my favorite scripture is?" she asked.

"Yes, Mom; it's *Hebrews 11:1 Now faith is the substance of things hoped for, the evidence of things unseen.* It was the first scripture that came to my mind when Dad told me the news of the cancer coming back."

"That's right, baby! You may not see the Lord but you know He is here; you may see this as the end but it's not. It's not goodbye; it's I'll see you later," she said as she cried and I cried.

"I love you, Mommy, and I don't want you to go!" I hugged her so tightly; weeping with my head on her chest.

"I love you too, Missy baby, with everything I have, and everything that I am. I'm always with you!" she said calmly as I laid in her arms all night.

I prayed myself to sleep. '*Dear Lord, Thank you for allowing me to have this beautiful soul as a mother. Thank you for her life and for you choosing her to be my mother. Help me to get through this Lord for she is going home to you. When you welcome her home, may she hear from you 'Well done thy good and faithful servant.' Thank you, Holy Spirit, for comforting my father and brother as well. I love you Lord and thank you! In Jesus mighty name! Amen!*'

The next morning I woke up with the early sunbeam shining through out the room and directly on my face. I heard the sound of the birds chirping outside and the water sprinklers. As I heard all these sounds around me there was something that I didn't hear: my mom's heartbeat. I sat up with a sick feeling inside as I looked up at her. She was sleeping but once I felt her neck for a pulse…she was gone! "AAAAAHHHH! MOMMMY! OH GOD!" I screamed. I put my hand over her face. My father and brother ran up the stairs and broke down crying once they got to the doorway. I've never seen my father cry so hard before; my brother was inconsolable.

Elaine and Qena came to the funeral in support and sat behind us at the church. The service was held at our family church Tabernacle Baptist were Ahmad and I got baptized; it was absolutely beautiful; I had never seen so many people. My mother looked like an angel with an all-white lace buttoned up to the neck long sleeve dress. She wore her pearl earrings; her hair was beautifully styled in a pixie cut by our family beautician. Her make-up was light with a touch of sandy gold MAC lip-gloss and her nails were manicured with clear nail polish. I bought her a corsage with yellow and white roses; I pinned it on the left side of her dress. She was loved, liked and honored in the way she deserved to be. All three of us managed to walk up to the podium and say thank you to everyone for being there. For their thoughts, cards, phone calls and prayers. My father and brother didn't say much and could barely stand up but they did what they could. I spoke about my mother's favorite scripture and the unconditional love she had for the Lord. The church members were great for helping us get everything in order. I was proud of my father, brother and my wonderful husband because we all pulled together to get everything done for her. It certainly was the hardest thing I've ever had to do; the Lord gave us the strength to endure and the Holy Spirit to guide us.

The repast was at my parent's house. Elaine and Qena were a big help in getting everything together including setting up the decorations and laying out the food; I couldn't have asked for better sisters. "Thank you both for being here!" I said to them as we were sitting on the couch after everyone had left.

"No need to thank us; we're supposed to be here but you're welcome," Qena said softly.

"You know—" Elaine said with a tear coming down her face—"she was like my second mom; I'm going to miss her so much!" she said as she started crying softly. I was sitting in the middle of them and I reached over to hug Elaine. I turned around and put my arm over Qena and we all engulfed in a group hug.

"She was one of a kind!" Qena said sweetly.

After everyone left, I was there alone in the house. My father went for a ride with Cory, my brother left with some friends and Elaine and Qena had to go back to their homes. It felt strange being there without knowing my mom wouldn't walk through the door. I sat in silence for a while and walked around the house; then I finally went upstairs to their bedroom and looked at the empty bed. I went to her vanity; looked through her jewelry and found a note pad with her handwriting on it. Then I went to her side of the closet and looked at her clothes, coats, furs and shoes. I opened the dresser drawer and pulled out a red blouse I've seen my mother wear. I held it tightly in my hands and walked out. Once I got in my room and sat on the bed, I brought the blouse up to my nose to smell… 'her scent.' I wept and cried so hard that I was starting to get a headache; I cried myself to sleep.

As the rain came down so did the tears; I was back at work and had to deal with grief. Everyone at the prescient showed their love and support; when I got to my desk, there were flowers and a card that everyone signed.

"Hey, Mist, it's good to see you and my deepest condolences to you and the family!" Terry said to me when he walked up to my desk. He's been keeping up with calls and checking in with my husband for information.

"Thank you so much for being in touch with us; it means a lot!" I said to him while wiping a few small tears from my check and gave him a hug.

"That's what friends are for; I wish I could've done more." he said.

"No! You've done enough and I'm so grateful for you!" I said to him.

Then Capt. Joshua came from behind and said, "Mist, my deepest sympathies. You did get my card, right?"

"Yes, Captain. I did and we appreciate it! I haven't had the time to write thank you cards to everyone but I will!" I said with a smile.

"No rush, Mist! As long as you know that we're here for you and the family!" Capt. Joshua said to me as he rubbed my back like a father. I smiled and nodded in agreement to his words of encouragement and they both walked away. I had to get my head right and I promised my mom that I would keep it together; it's tough but I will survive.

The next two weeks I poured myself into the case. I saw all the names of the officers that were there; to see my father's name gave me a warm feeling inside. However, I knew that I would need to go back home and check something's out with my dad in toe with me. I had used all of my sick and bereavement time with helping my mother so I had to find another way or should I say God has to find a way for me!

"Suspended! Why, Captain?" I asked in anger trying not to raise my voice.

"You're getting beside yourself; becoming obsessed," Capt. Joshua said.

"What's wrong with me trying to solve this case?" I asked in confusion.

"You're ignoring the ones you have here! I need you to get these done first!" Capt. Joshua said.

"IGNORING!" I said loudly. "This one still hasn't been solved yet and I'm on the brink of closing it! You can't pull me out now!" I said full of fury. "Yes, I can and I will! I'm going to let the North Carolina department handle it—"

"WHAT!" I shouted; Capt. Joshua continued not paying attention.

"I know it's personal but that's the thing; I can't let you drop everything for your own personal dealings with that case!" Capt. Joshua said and he was starting to get riled up.

"So, how did it end up on my desk in the first place?" I asked getting pissed off.

"I don't know! That's something I'm trying to find out but as of now back off, Misty!" Capt. Joshua said as if he was warning me.

I was flaming hot! So hot you could've cooked an egg on my head. I had to bring it down a notch because I didn't want him to know what I was going to do next; I just went with it. "You're the most passionate person that I've had the pleasure to meet, Misty. I know your mother's passing is still fresh and you've been handling yourself well but I can't have you on this case. I'm sorry!" Capt. Joshua said genuinely.

I was silent for a moment. Thinking about how long I've been waiting and how I knew in my bones that this assignment was appointed to me. I recognized that this was a *blessing* in disguise. All of the sudden; I felt peace in my spirit with the decision I was going to have to make. I looked at him dead in his eyes for a moment and said,

"Thank you, Captain, for all you have done for me. *I'm out*!"

Chapter 10
Romans 8:31

"Dad! You and I are going to finally solve this case together!" I said full of excitement as we both sat on the couch in my parent's living room.

"Misty, I'm honored! I can't believe you walked away from the station!" he said laughing and a little confused.

"I can always go back; just not at that precinct but I have a plan! I want to start my own detective services for cold cases! I've been thinking about this for a while now; praying and fasting and I know it's the right time!" I said excitedly.

"Misty, I know how stubborn you can be but I'm so proud of you; that sounds awesome!" He said happily. It's the first time since my mom's passing that I've heard him sound hopeful.

"Yes, Dad! I want you and I to be partners! Work with me!" He wasn't all the way sold. "Ever since mom's transition I've been thinking about how to get you back into action. I can't have you walking around like a zombie; you're still in the land of the living!" I said.

"I'm older now, Misty. What can I do? It sounds good but these old bones aren't ready for a showdown," he said. I wasn't backing down.

"I understand, Dad; I know you still have adventure left in you! It's time for you to step up and get back into the game! Everyone handles grief differently." I had to take a moment to consider my father's feelings. "You don't think I miss Mommy!" I said as my voice started to crack and a tear fell down. "I think about her with every breath in my body and I know she would be thrilled! She would support this movement," I said softly as my dad looked at me deep in my eyes; I saw his eyes water for a brief moment.

"I need you, Dad. What's that scripture you would always say when obstacles would come up?" I asked.

He took a moment, smiled at me and said, *"If God be for us, who can be against us? Romans 8:31!"*

"I rest my case!" I said. We laughed and hugged each other tightly. With God, we came into an agreement as a family to finally put *this* case that's long overdue to rest.

The next morning we went to the station and pulled the box from the cold case area that contained the files along with the physical evidence and went to work. Sure enough there were only two bullet shells. The photos I had were copies but the ones in the case box were the originals. We both saw the specks of blood on the inside of the driver seat on the right side! "You can't really see it with the naked eye because the seats where burgundy color as well and it blended it in! That's why I had to get my magnifying glass to take a closer look! I took the photo to the blood splatter experts and they confirmed it was in fact blood! No bullet hole in the seat because the seat was pulled back and when

Winston was driving, he was sitting up; leaning more toward the steering wheel! The bullet that came through the trunk hit him in the back most likely in the right shoulder blade! Those last shots from Officer Byrd's gun when Winston drove off was a last attempt to single him out if he was ever caught. I believe it was done with that intention; Officer Byrd while dying made his last cry for help!" I said with confidence.

"Baby girl, you're a star! I haven't looked at these files in years; it's a wonder what you can see when you go back and look again with a different perspective. I was so drunk with revenge trying to find out who did this to my friends I really didn't take in the paperwork or the evidence. Officer Byrd and I joined the force together; that's why it really hit home," he said.

"You never told me that, Dad—" I paused for a moment to think about what he said—"I never even thought to ask you how you knew them," I said fondly.

"Yes, Officer Byrd and I met in the academy like you and Qena; Officer Scott was my first field officer."

"Dad, that's wonderful; I'm very happy to hear this!" I said.

"I'll talk to you about them another time. Let's get busy and make some calls!" Andrew located Detective John Hill. He's now living in Houston, Texas and works at the states police department. He received John's cell phone number from the prescient and gives him a call.

"Hello, John! How are you; it's been a long time? I got your number from the prescient; was that okay?" Andrew asked.

"Hey, man! Wow; it has been long time! Sure, it's okay, old friend! I'm good; how are you?" John asked.

"I'm okay. I've been retired for a while now. You know I just lost my wife a month ago," Andrew said.

"Oh, Andrew man. I'm so sorry to hear that! My condolences; Inez was a treasure! How are the kids?" John asked instinctively.

"Thanks, John! Kids! You mean grown adults!" Andrew said laughing.

"Right! Time sure does fly!" John said laughing.

"Yeah! Misty is a detective herself now; married and Ahmad is an engineer at NASA."

Andrew said proudly.

"That's incredible! I know you and Inez are proud that your children are doing well!" John said genuinely.

"Yes; it's by the grace of God and I'm very proud! How's your wife, Tamron, and the kids?" Andrew asked jokingly while laughing.

"Wife is good and yeah speaking of adults I should've known mine are too! Kendall is an RN and Torrance Todd works for the city of Houston as a garbage man. I plan on retiring myself next year!" John said proudly as well.

"That's alright, man! Glad you and your family are well. I wanted to ask you about the case with Scott and Byrd. I know it's been a long time; have you found out anything else about it?" Andrew asked curiously.

"Yeah, Drew, we really tried to bring this case the justice it deserves. I found out Winston has a son—"

"WHAT!" Andrew yelled in shock.

"YEP!" John continued. "My wife Tamron has a best friend named Bella. Bella had an aunt named Esther who ran a day care back in the day; she used to help women that were struggling and would watch some of the kids for free. My wife told me that Bella became good friends with a girl named Frances; they worked at a coffee shop together. Bella referred Frances to her aunt's day care because she needed the help with her son and how the baby's father was a criminal named Winston. She showed Bella a picture of herself and Winston as a couple when Frances was pregnant. Frances moved away but still kept in contact with Aunt Esther until she didn't hear from her anymore.

"Seven years later when we put out the composite sketch drawing of the suspect for the double homicide case Bella tells my wife that he was the guy in Frances' picture; his name is Winston! Bella told me the last place Frances was staying at but she was long gone. No family. Nothing and it became a dead end!" John said.

"WHOA! What's the kid's name?" Andrew asked hastily.

"I think his name is Carl! He may be the same age as Misty!" John said.

"That's why her name isn't in the flies; she left before he committed the murders," Andrew said, his old self was starting to show up again.

"YEP! It's a small world, isn't it?" John said.

"Too small! Everything we needed was floating all around us and didn't even know it! Thanks, John, you're a life saver!" Andrew said full of gratitude.

"My pleasure, Drew! Keep me posted when you do find his son!"

"You got it! I'll come visit and we can go on a fishing trip once you retire; how about that old friend?" Andrew asked smiling.

"Sounds like a plan! Make sure you write my number down!" John said.

"I'll save it in my contacts and I will text you mines as well! Thanks again, John!" Andrew said.

"Anytime!" He hung up the phone.

"Winston has a *son,* Misty!" my dad said to me in disbelief.

"John said his name is Carl!" Andrew said.

"WOW! I was speechless for a moment. Let's keep looking maybe he has Winston's last name; Poe! I'll look up Carl Poe!" I said with excitement. I searched the computer engines, papers; everything! There wasn't any more leads! It's been hours and we still couldn't find anything with Carl Poe's name on it!

"I think we'll try again tomorrow, Missy. It's getting late and we should call it a night," Andrew said as he was standing up and stretching.

"I'm okay, Dad. I'll stay for a while; it's only 7 o'clock!" I said. "I know once you get started, there's no turning back. You get it from your old man! Okay, please be careful."

My dad leaned down and kissed my forehead. "I love you," he said.

"Love you too, Dad!" I called Cory to let him know that I was going to stay a little longer at the station and I kept digging. After about an hour, I was done. I felt something in my spirit to go visit the crime scene; I didn't ever think about going before.

I said to myself, '*I know it's dark but I'll be fine; I have my piece on me!*' I sat contemplating for a couple of minutes. Then with this fire inside of me I jumped up, grabbed my blazer and said, "*I'm going!*"

I underestimated how dark it really gets in North Carolina. It was dead dark with only the headlights lighting the road. I said to myself, '*I'm an idiot for even coming here but I have to!*' My soul has been tingling to come and I needed to see it; there it was: Holt Road. I pulled behind the small street sign, turned the car off and left my headlights on. I had a flashlight with me as well. I checked to make sure my gun had a live round available and stuck it on the side my hip. When I stepped out of the car, I felt a mighty rushing wind next to me, blowing my hair against my face as if it was the Holy Spirit leading me forward. As I was walking on the side of the road with my flashlight I walked up to where it was a big hole in the middle of the road. I stopped there and looked all around to see if anyone was behind me. I began to see a vision as if the Lord was showing me exactly what happened; from the outside looking into the scene.

Officer Scott and Officer Byrd where in the car; they had turned on their signal lights for Winston to stop. They then pulled up behind the burgundy Cadillac. Officer Byrd got out first. He was Black, medium height 5'8", athletic frame, light skinned with jet-black short hair. Officer Scott was Caucasian with sandy blonde hair, blue eyes, medium height 5'7" with an athletic frame too. Officer Scott followed suite and got out after his partner. He walked over and stood at the backseat of the passenger side of the Cadillac. Officer Byrd walked up to the driver side. "You were driving pretty fast; can I see your driver's license and registration?" Officer Byrd asked Winston.

"Yes, sir!" a young Winston answered quickly. While Officer Byrd looked at him, he could see the terror and guilt in his face; he could sense Winston was lying.

"Step out of the car right now!" Officer Byrd told Winston with authority. As Winston started to get out of the car, he quickly grabbed his gun from his waist! Officer Byrd saw it and reached for his gun at the same time but Winston got to his first and shot twice!

BOOM! BOOM!

Officer Byrd fell down! Officer Scott ran back to the police passenger car door; opened it and started shooting using the door as a shield.

BOOM! BOOM!

Missing Winston as he was ducking on the side of the Cadillac. Officer Scott retreated back into the car to call for help. When the coast was clear, Winston ran up to the car and started shooting endlessly; emptying out his gun hitting Officer Scott with multiple gunshots wounds killing him instantly! Winston ran back to the car, got in and drove away. Officer Byrd with his last breath sat up and shot three times at the car!

BOOM! BOOM! BOOM!

Two shots hit the back window and the last shot hit the trunk! Winston stopped abruptly; realizing he was hit! I could hear footsteps coming from behind. Before I could turn around someone grabbed me; put a cloth of over my mouth and everything went black!

As I slowly opened my eyes from being drugged, I was looking at lamp on a desk. I was lying on my side and when I turned around very slothfully my vision started to come into focus; I saw Charlie sitting in a chair! I sat up so quick you would've thought a fire was coming.

"CHARLIE! WHAT THE HELL IS GOING ON? WHERE AM I?" I screamed at him with anger and confusion.

"Misty! Please calm down. I'll tell you everything. I need you to remain calm! I know it looks bad! I'm sorry I had to abduct you but I had no choice," Charlie said with guilt.

I sat and listened to him; I tried to get my nerves under control. I knew he wouldn't hurt me; I had that feeling. I nodded and gave him a scowl look in agreement for him to get busy explaining himself.

"My name is Charlie Winston Baker!" Charlie said with dignity. My eyes were getting ready to come out of the sockets when I recognized his middle name.

I gasped, "OH MY GOD!"

Charlie held up his hand signaling me to allow him to finish.

"Before I graduated high school my mom told me about my real father; Winston Poe! During college I became obsessive about the case; reading newspaper articles and seeing the names of the officers and detectives that were there; I made sure to remember them! After graduating I made the decision to become a police officer; what my father did inspired me to pursue a career in law enforcement and also so I could get access to the unauthorized files with the details. In the file I saw your father's name again along with his picture. I read where my father was last seen and it was in Mexico City!"

"A couple of years later I moved to New York for a fresh start and became a detective. I worked at the 23rd precinct and transferred to 54th. I'd been there only a week when I felt it was time for me to go on a personal manhunt to find my father. I went on vacation to Mexico City; I miraculously found him by the grace of God by a chance encounter with a housekeeping maid named Coco at the resort I was staying at. When she saw me, she knew who my father was because the resemblance was undeniable. She used to housekeep at the hotel where he was hiding out at and she helped him! She gave me his last known address; I went and met my father face to face for the first time in my life. He was regretful and knew he needed to turn himself in. We agreed he would come to New York and settle in with me until I figured out a way to help him. The day that I met you and you said your full name I went into panic mode! I remembered your father's name: *Andrew Rivers*! I couldn't believe it!" I said to myself, '*I feel a sense of relief; I can finally tell someone about this secret I've been keeping and she might understand since both of our fathers are involved.'*

"Then that same night when I got home, my father left me a note saying he was coming back here! I've been back for five weeks and I still can't find him! So, I called and asked for your information at our precinct. I followed you and your father to the station and once I saw you leave, I figured you would go to Holt road," Charlie said.

I couldn't do anything but listen with my heart. I thought to myself, *'what would Jesus do? What would I do if I were in his position?'* I felt bad for him because he was torn in between this unfortunate situation but God in His ultimate wisdom turned it around for good! The word tells us in *Romans 8:28 That all things work together for good to them that love God* and Charlie was trying his best to make things work out. He does know the risk especially being in law enforcement but he put it all on the line to try and repent for the sins of his father. At that moment I recognized that I'm supposed to help! I looked at him and said, "You're the one who put the file on my desk; the name that was blacked out in the report and your name isn't Carl! I said inquisitively. How did you do all of this without anyone noticing?" I asked curiously.

"The night I found out my dad fled, I came into the station early the next morning and left the file without anyone batting an eye! I kept everything under the radar; did my job and made sure not to seem suspicious. No one had a clue!" Charlie answered.

"WOW!" I said shaking my head in disbelief. I took a deep breath and said, "Charlie, I understand exactly where you're coming from and I know how it could be extremely difficult to not be able to talk to somebody! Honestly, I might've done the same thing!" I said to him wholeheartedly. "It all makes sense now and we can do it together! Next time please don't kidnap me; I was scared out of my mind!" I said with a warm genuine smile. Charlie smiled too. "You know…I became obsessed too! My father almost killed himself over this case and it was my prayer to help him! It's amazing how we're both one in the same; how God weaved it into His perfect design!" I said as we smiled at each other.

I could see the stress leave Charlie's face after this conversation. I thought to myself, '*He needed someone and I'm glad the Lord chose me to be that somebody who he could trust.*' As I scooted down to the end of the bed to stand up, I said, "Now, let's go and find your father!" Charlie nodded and stood up. We both walked to the door and as he opened it, we were greeted with;

"Hello, Son!" Winston said as he held a gun to Charlie and myself. "Nobody is going to look for me because I'm already here! Get back inside!" Winston said with force. He held the gun closer to Charlie's chest. As we both slowly walked back into the room, he searched us and took both of our guns and laid them on the table. He told us to grab the two chairs and sit down; we were sitting side by side. He took the extension cord from the hotel phone and told me to tie up Charlie's hands behind his back while he held the gun to my face. He then told me to take Charlie's shoelaces and mines out. Winston put his gun on the side of his waist; quickly grabbed the laces and tied my hands in front of me and tied my feet together. My phone was blowing up in my pocket but I couldn't reach it to answer. After he was done tying; he stood up over us. He went to peer out the window to see if anyone had followed him. I looked over at Charlie and then my eyes darted behind him. I saw him pull out a pocketknife from behind his back out from the waist of his pants; he seemed to keep it there for just in case purposes such as this!

"Same 'ole Winston Poe! You don't wanna change! What type of man pulls a gun on his child? That's not a man; that a coward!" While Charlie was talking, he was vigorously cutting trying to distract Winston from what he was doing. He continued. "You disgust me! I hate that I have your blood running through my veins!" Charlie said spitefully. I sat in silence trying to pick the knots in the shoelaces with my fingertips but he tied them really tight. I wasn't going to give up; if I kept doing it without Winston noticing I could break free.

"You're right, Son—"

"I'm NOT your son!" Charlie said with hatred. Winston looked at him like he was about to smack him but he didn't.

"I can't change! I thought I wanted to turn myself in and do right by you since I've never done right by anybody; not even myself. I told you it's been too long and I don't want to live out the rest of my days in prison—"

"YOU KIILED TWO PEOPLE!" Charlie yelled. "They didn't get the chance to live or watch their kids grow up!" Charlie said angrily.

"HOW DARE YOU!" I shouted. "You ruined a lot of lives, Winston—"

"SHUT UP YOU!" He yelled as he turned to face me. "YOU know nothing about anything!" Winston said. He then turned around and lifted up his shirt; revealing an old gash, a scar on his right shoulder blade; it was the bullet wound! Charlie and I looked closely and we were both shocked! By this time I looked behind Charlie and he almost cut all of the cords off!

Winston turned back around to face us. "That's right! The officer did hit me! To tell you the truth I didn't think I would ever get caught! I lied, Son. I didn't give a damn about those officers and really, I don't give a damn about you either!" Winston said viciously with hate in his eyes.

Before he could say another word, Charlie broke free, dropped the knife in front of me on the floor and charged at his father! They were wrestling as Charlie was holding Winston's arm up trying to shake the gun from his hand. They fell on the bed with Winston on top and then Charlie turned him around so that he was on top. I grabbed the knife and finally managed to cut through the shoelaces around my hands and feet; then I heard the gun go off!

BOOM!

Winston had thrown Charlie to the ground! I ran to the table where the guns were; grabbed one and turned around! Winston took a shot at me.

BOOM!

It missed and hit the window! I Shot!

BOOM! BOOM!

Hitting Winston in the left shoulder and arm; he dropped the gun! I didn't want to kill him because I wanted him to stand trial for what he has done and killing Winston would be the easy way out. I ran up and retrieved his gun. I went to Charlie and checked for a pulse on his neck; he was still alive! The door busted open, "BAM!" With the S.W.A.T. police and my father right along with them!

There were a couple of ambulances and a dozen police cars all over the parking lot. The stretcher brought Charlie out first with an oxygen mask over his face. I walked up to look at him then I nodded for the paramedic to take him inside the A-car. I looked over and saw the second stretcher with Winston; he was loud, abrasive and acting a fool even while being shot. "LET ME GO DAMMIT! SHE SHOT ME! LET ME GO DAMMIT!" He looked pathetic. They had him handcuffed while lying on the stretcher.

My father came and stood right next to me and asked in a father's tone, "Are you okay, baby girl?" I nodded in a yes gesture. I turned to look at him while he was still staring at Winston, he looked satisfied; I could finally see peace on his face. He turned around and looked me directly in the eyes and said, "I'm so proud of you. I don't know what I would do if something were to happen to my children; you and Ahmad are all I have! Thank you for helping your old man! I love you, Misty!"

Looking back at him with a tear about to fall from my eye I said softly, "I love you too, Dad." We hugged tightly. After the embrace I asked, "Dad, how did you find us?"

"I tracked your phone, baby girl! I may be retired but I'm still a detective at heart and don't you ever forget it!" he said laughing and pointing at my nose. He hugged me again tightly and we laughed. As we started walking to his car he added, "And I've been doing this since before you were born, Missy Pooh!" We laughed!

Chapter 11
Nothing Is Impossible

"Guilty of capital murder. The defendant, Winston Luke Poe, is sentenced to two consecutive life sentences without the possibility of parole," Judge Aveeno said in court. While my father and I were listening to the sentencing of Mr. Winston Poe, I heard the Lord whisper His word; *Luke 1:37 Nothing is Impossible with God.* Proof that no matter how long it takes or the detours life will take you rest assured God is always on time!

Winston was sitting in a wheelchair; he didn't look at us not once. I couldn't believe how he tried to act like he was feeble. Not too long ago he was an action figure now that he's in prison his trying to get some sympathy. What really took the cake was when the judge asked him if he had anything to say. He stood up and began speaking then started to cry. Was he really remorseful or was this all an act because he was caught? As a woman of God, I have to have compassion for him because no matter what he's still God's child. However, he told me he didn't care about who he hurt so how do you know if a person is truly regretful for what they have done? It took decades for this moment to happen and he had no intentions of coming forward. Jesus said it's not my will but God's will be done! In the end he has to take that up with the Lord; my job is to forgive and not worry about the rest.

After he was finished the bailiff received the okay to take him into custody and wheel him to the back; court was adjourned. I thought to myself, *'you waited your whole life for a single moment and finally that day comes!'* As my dad and I stood up to leave he turned to me and said, "Well, baby girl, that's it! It's all over! I can't believe I get to actually say those words. I feel that justice was finally served for my friends. Their lives were not taken in vain because we didn't give up on them!"

Just then, two women came up to us and my father knew immediately who they were. They both hugged him and then he turned around and said, "Missy baby, these are the widows of Officer Brian Scott and Officer Eddie Byrd. This is Mrs. Trisha Scott." She was a tall, pretty brunette Caucasian woman. "And this is Mrs. Zayla Byrd," he said. She was medium height with brown sugar skin; lovely woman with brown hair. This was my first time ever meeting them and it warmed my heart.

They both gave me a hug; while smiling and shedding some tears Mrs. Trisha said, "We've heard a lot about you Misty, and it's a pleasure to finally meet you! I thank you both so much for all that you have done. Andrew, I want to thank you for being here and always keeping in contact with our family."

"Misty, you're an exceptional young woman! Andrew, I thank you too! For being there for our family as well. You both don't know how much this means to Trisha and I. We've become an extended family and I know Eddie would have wanted this," Mrs. Zayla said with love. I was crying with tears of joy; I felt the Holy Spirit bring us together. I couldn't speak only reach out and hug them; then we all came in for one big embrace.

Charlie survived. The bullet missed his heart and came through making it a clean exit wound not hitting any major arteries. Once he was finished in recovery he was booked and charged with holding a fugitive. My father and I went to his sentencing too. When the bailiff brought him out, he looked good! You could tell that a weight has been lifted from him; even his eyes seem filled with light and hope. He knew that he would have to sacrifice his career and he was okay with that decision. "One year in prison along with one-year probation Mr. Baker and it pains for me to do this but I have to revoke your badge. You were a fine detective and I wish you well in your future career endeavors." Judge Wang said in court as Charlie was standing and nodded. When the judge was finished, Charlie turned around to see his parents and to his surprise he saw my father and I standing in the back. He was so happy to see us his eyes were smiling. I believe he felt the love and support from us as we both smiled and nodded in acceptance of him.

A few days after his sentencing I went to visit Charlie alone at the Whitmire Correctional facility in Greensboro, North Carolina. I was able to have a physical visit and not between the class. I was a little concerned about his mindset because he has been through a lot of emotional distress; only by the grace of God he made it through. Charlie gets to have a clean slate just like what Jesus did for us when he shed his blood; it washed away our sins for us to have a new life. When the guard brought him out, I stood up from my chair. He saw me and smiled a sweet smile along with a look of confusion. He walked over to his chair that was across from mines and we both sat down.

"Hey! What are you doing here? I mean; I'm glad you're here!" he said nervously.

"I'm glad I'm here too! It was in my spirit to come and check on you! How've you been holding up?" I asked.

"It's not as bad as I thought it was going to be," he said. "I'm grateful for my family's support; that's keeping me sane." Then he looked me straight in the eyes and said sincerely, "Thank you, Misty! I don't think I could've done this without you."

"This was all God's plan. I couldn't have done it without Him nor without you either!"

"Thank *you*, Charlie!" Then I took a moment and asked, "Do you know the Lord?"

"My parents took me to church but once I got older, I drifted away until the night before I met Coco. I prayed for the first time in years and asked God to help me and He did! I would like to get to know God more," he said.

"Are you a believer in Jesus Christ? Do you know anything about Him?" I asked.

"I do know of Him but I don't have a strong relationship as I should," he said.

"Then say this prayer with me." I held out both of my hands for him to hold, we bowed our heads and I said to

Charlie, "Repeat this prayer with me. '*Father God of Heaven and Earth we ask for your forgiveness of our sins'*. He repeated.

"Father God of heaven and earth we ask for your forgiveness of our sins." *We repent for the kingdom of Heaven is at hand.* He repeated, "We repent for the kingdom of Heaven is at hand. *I believe Jesus Christ came to earth as a man, showed us the way, the truth and the life.*" He repeated, "I believe Jesus Christ came to earth as a man, showed us the way, the truth and the life. *I believe that He died and rose again on the third day with all power in his hand.* He repeated, I believe that He died and rose again on the third day with all power in his hand. *I accept Jesus Christ as my Lord and Savior and I give my life to him.* He repeated, "I accept Jesus Christ as my Lord and Savior and I give my life to him. *Thank you, Lord, for saving me; thank you, Lord, for loving me. Thank you; Lord, for a new beginning! In Jesus name, thank God! Amen!*" He repeated "Thank you Lord for saving me, thank you Lord for loving me. Thank you Lord, for a new beginning! In Jesus name, thank God! Amen!"

"You did it!" I said to him when we both opened our eyes! I continued. "Make sure you keep up your relationship with Him by going to church services in here and when you're home; you can even come to my church if you like! Going to Bible study will teach you about fasting, praying and love; it will connect you more to God's word. Congratulations on your new relationship with Jesus Christ and now you can start living for HIM!" I told Charlie with love.

"Wow, I will! I didn't know it was that easy; all I had to do was repent, believe in Jesus and rededicate my life to the Lord. That's why God has His angels on earth to be able to lead me back to Him; I thank God for them and for *you*, Misty! Thank you so much!" he said with hope.

"That's my job! I may be a detective but I work for the Lord first!" I said with confidence holding up my index finger indicating the number #1. "And speaking of work once you finish your stint here, I may have a job for you; I'm going to start my own detective firm with my father! How about it? Would you like to work with me?" I asked with enthusiasm. Charlie's eyes lit up and I could see excitement in them.

"You don't have to ask me twice! I'll be honored to work with you!" he said gleefully.

"TIMES UP!" the guard blurted out.

As we stood up, I said, "Then it's on!"

"BET!" Charlie said and we shared a short platonic hug. As I was standing there watching him walk away, I thought to myself, '*the enemy wants you to think you're alone but you're not!*' We all have our own crosses to bear and the word tells us in *Hebrews 10:24–25 And let us consider how we may spur one another on toward love and good deeds, not giving up meeting together, as some are in the habit of doing, but encouraging one another.* We're supposed to be there for those in the time of need. I said to myself, '*Thank you God; you have another soul!*'

195

"What are you guys doing here?" I said in shock to Elaine and Qena as I opened the door to my parent's house! We hugged and laughed falling all over each other.

"Well, I called Qena and asked her if she wanted to come to Fayetteville so we could surprise you! We know you have been superwoman lately and we're so happy you and your dad are okay!" Elaine said.

"We just wanted to let you know that we're here for you, we love you and it's time to have a little fun! I'm only here for two days and since I'm back in your hometown, let's get the party started!" Qena said.

"I'm so happy you guys came! Thank you so much. It means a lot to me that you both feel that way. Oh, and you're just in time because I wanted to go check out this comedy show at the Blaze Theatre tonight at 8:30!" I said.

"Yesss! Let's hurry up we only have an hour for all of us to get dressed and you know Elaine takes the longest to get ready!" Qena said crossing her arms.

"I do, I do! That's because I believe in perfection okay! Let's get it!" Elaine said. We had a ladies' night out on the town! When we got back to my parents' house, we had an old school slumber party and laughed our faces off for the rest of the night.

A few days after the girls left the house was empty. I had spoken to my husband to remind him that I'll be coming home soon in case he forgot what I looked like! My dad went to play poker with his friends and Ahmad was out as well. I had a chance to walk around the house and admire my mother's handy work. Looking at her china cabinet, her aprons, recipe cards, and the wallpaper she chose throughout house. The rug she picked out in the family room, all of the pictures she had meticulously placed because she wanted everything just right. Her presence was very much alive as it should be. I walked upstairs to my parent's room and looked into the closet. Her side was still there in tact; I know my father wants to leave it the way it was before she left. I sat there looking at all of her belongs again this time with a different feeling. I sensed it was time to start packing up but I am keeping the mink coat along with a few trinkets!

I would also give Elaine and Qena something since they are like my sisters; I know my mom would love that. It's been a couple months and I'm okay; it has to be done sooner or later. I will give my father all the time he needs within reason. I walked back down stairs, grabbed my purse off of the coat rack and headed to the cemetery.

I visited my grandma first. I kneeled down and put purple lilies on her headstone; that was her favorite flower. I smiled as I thought about the way she made me feel and it still tickles me today. I'm a part of her tree and it made me feel good inside; I said a prayer and kissed the sky. Then I went to my mother's grave, which wasn't that far away. I brought her favorite flower, sunflowers and put them on her headstone. Sadness suddenly came over me; her passing was still fresh. I started to cry and as the tears came down that same mighty rushing wind came again like it did when I was at Holt Road. I felt something; as if it was my mom's hand brushing against my left cheek to wipe the tears from my eye. It was the most comforting feeling I've had since her transition. The Lord allowed her to let me know she's with me; like Jesus is! He set the example in which both my grandma and mom are a part of now and one day I'll have to follow. I know without a shadow of a doubt they are with Him! My tears instantly turned into joy. Although, I miss their physical presence terribly I'll see them again. I said to myself with confidence, '*It's not goodbye; it's I'll see you later, Missy baby!*'

At the airport I could tell my dad was sad that I was leaving. "Got everything you need?" he asked while we were waiting for my plane to board.

"Yes, Daddy!" I said and continued, "I've got everything except *YOU* but you'll be coming to New York soon! Ahmad will be here for another week and I'm glad you aren't home alone most of the time."

"After he leaves you know I'm coming out! We're partners and we need to plan our next adventure!" my dad said with excitement.

"Yes, and we can travel too, Dad, that'll be one for the history books! What'd you think?" I asked him waiting for his response.

He took out his hand for me to shake and said lovingly, "Sounds like a plan, detective! I love you."

I took out my hand and shook his and said, "I love you too, Dad!" We embraced and said prayers for traveling mercies. The flight attendant called for boarding over the intercom: "GATE 8 FLIGHT 227 IS READY TO BOARD NOW!"

"That's me, Dad!" I said. We hugged tightly again and he semi lifted me off the ground.

"Ummmah!" I gave him a big kiss on the cheek! When I turned around to walk onto the plane, I had a revelation and thought to myself, '*This is the beginning of a whole new chapter in my life. When God closes one door, He always opens another and I can't wait to see what's next!*'

Acknowledgment

Thank you, Lord, for pouring out your Holy Spirit and giving me another gift that I didn't know I had. I love you Jesus! To the one and only Mrs. Joyce Ann; my mommy. Your love is deeper than unconditional and I thank you for always being real. Thank you for constantly reminding me of the endless possibilities of working with what I have and that it's more than enough! You're the reason along with God that this story was brought to life and I thank you. I love you mommy! To my late father, Richard Andrew Grundy, I love you! To my big sis, Shavonda Hayden, I love you! To all my family and friends; those who have passed on and most that are still here thank you for loving and keeping me lifted throughout my life's journey. I love you all!

Special thank you.

To my big cousin, Officer John Gardenhire for over 30 years of police service to the community and for helping me with information for this book! Thank you! I love you! To my cousin, Bishop Alvin Moore Sr., for your love and support! Thank you for believing in me from the start! I love you! To the late Officer Shiree Lejin Arrant who was the first female police officer I ever knew that displayed strength and femininity in service and motherhood; I miss and love you! To the Late Anthony L White who was my father figure. He didn't get the chance to see the book come into fruition but was the first to print out the manuscript. I thank God I had the chance to tell him that it was going to be published! I miss and love you! Thank you, Austin Macauley Publishers, for believing in this story. Until next time, always remember; God is perfect!

Printed in the USA
CPSIA information can be obtained
at www.ICGtesting.com
LVHW021330050224
770959LV00001B/133

9 781685 628819